DEAR MR. CLAUS,

I've got Nintendo and G.I. Joe and a lot of other stuff, so I'm not asking for toys this year. Do you bring trees? Dad bought this metal thing instead—he says it's art and I guess it must be 'cause it sure ain't a real Christmas tree. I'd like a tree just like the one Leah's got at her house. Leah's tree has tons of tinsel and a zillion ornaments, and when you visit her, you never have to worry about accidentally breaking any art.

When you bring the tree to our house, could you tell my dad something? Lately I've been thinking about having a mom. A mom would make Christmas cookies and cocoa and help my dad pick a really big Christmas tree. Could you tell Dad I've been thinking about that? 'Cause maybe he's been thinking about it, too.

Meet one of the seven winners of the American Romance Christmas Is For Kids Photo Contest, whose likeness appears on the cover of *The Best Gift of All*. He is Alex Mims of Charleston, South Carolina.

His mom and dad, Jennifer and James Mims, wrote to tell us of Alex's excitement and anticipation of Christmas morning. They say:

Alex was so excited about Santa Claus coming that when Christmas morning came, he opened the presents in his stocking and was overjoyed. He was ready to eat breakfast until we told him to look under the tree. He was surprised to find even more gifts there for him.

THE BEST GIFT OF ALL

ANDREA DAVIDSON

Harlequin Books

TORONTO • NEW YORK • LONDON
AMSTERDAM • PARIS • SYDNEY • HAMBURG
STOCKHOLM • ATHENS • TOKYO • MILAN

Published December 1989

First printing October 1989

ISBN 0-373-16324-X

Chapter One

Eight-year-old Spencer Carruthers advanced cautiously around the left side of the bronze monstrosity. "It doesn't look like a Christmas tree," he said.

Grandpa Pop, his nose twitching like a rabbit in a patch of skunkweed, angled around the other side. "Dudn't much smell like one, neither."

They met in front of it and, seeking authority and explanation, turned to the boy's father. Mark Carruthers signed the requisite delivery forms and paid the two burly hulks who had just deposited the sculpture in his living room. Not yet ready to face the inevitable puzzlement of his son and his father, he accompanied the two men to the front door. A light freezing drizzle had fallen during the morning, and the sound of spinning tires on slick pavement could be heard at the end of the broad, tree-lined avenue. Live oaks. Forever green. Even in the dead of winter.

Like a befuddled adolescent, the city of Edgeton hung at the very skirt of Blue Mountain, as if the town longed to break free but wasn't yet ready to cut the apron strings. Steel high-rise office buildings strove ever higher, aiming skyward, aspiring to tower over the rolling hills to the east. But, despite all valiant efforts, the town never quite gained the autonomy it so desperately sought. It clung still to the mountain. Over the years the townspeople and the hill people had grown progressively hostile toward one another, denying right to each other's territory and, even in some instances, like a house divided, denying blood kinship.

Mark had been trying all his life to sever his ties with the mountain and its people. He had built his four-thousand-square-foot contemporary on the far side of Edgeton, where the view from his front yard was a panorama of glass and steel, a veritable vista of upward and onward advancement. The high-rise buildings blocked all view of the mountains to the east, which was just the way he wanted it. He wanted no reminders of where he had come from.

He closed the front door and came into the living room to face the quizzical looks of his son and father.

He would hold onto his patience. "It's art nouveau."

"Art?" Spencer scowled at the thing and pulled on his lower lip. Last week in fourth period, Mrs. Merkle made a big deal of hanging up Timmy Berkstrom's drawing of a turbo-powered fighter jet complete with missiles and harpoons. An awesome plane. Now *that* was art. But this thing...

Grandpa Pop pulled a stubby pigtailed cigar from his pocket and gave it a good lick before slipping it between his teeth. "Yep," he said, working his mouth around the fat stogie, "figured it was somethin' like that. Knew t'weren't a Christmas tree. Knew that right off. Yep, son, I figured it was some kind of art. Y' remember old Uncle Louie that worked at Cus'n Duck's weldin' shop?"

Mark shifted his attention away from his father and cast an admiring glance at the sculpture. "This is a Leicester. He's well-known in quite a few circles." The declaration was meant to nip the older man's reminiscence before it had a chance to bud. He didn't want to hear anything about Uncle Louie or Cousin Duck or any of the other five hundred and forty-three relatives who still idled like bloated ticks over the backside of Blue Mountain.

"Abel claims he's the up-and-coming Calder," added Mark to his unappreciative audience. "We're buying several of his pieces for the office."

"Musta been when y' were about ten or so," mumbled Pop, unaware, as usual, that his son wasn't paying attention to him. "Back in sixty-six, I reckon..."

Mark peered at his watch, then looked over at Spencer. The boy was exploring the tree with an intensity that Mark found fascinating. Poking, prodding, probing into intricacies that only an eight-year-old mind could appreciate. Spencer Jacob Carruthers was a product of genes that defied all attempts to be labeled. Mark had tried to mold his son into his own image, he really had. Just as he had been molded by others. But there was a touch of wildfire in the boy that Mark had been unable to contain. It was those eyes of Spencer's, eyes that looked like the morning sky over Blue Mountain, and that mass of white-blond hair that fought every attempt of the barber's talents.

It was the hills, Mark thought ruefully. Spencer was a constant reminder of them. No matter how fast and hard Mark had run, he was still tethered to the mountain. He couldn't leave behind the running, barefoot boy. He couldn't escape his past.

Spencer was still investigating the big bronze thing and, unbeknownst to his father, was about to determine that a few inconspicuous twists and bends in the metal were all that was needed to turn the sculpture into a radical clubhouse.

Staring at the art form and still rambling on was Pop. "Well, Old Uncle Louie he took him a bunch of scrap tail pipes and he welded them into the durndest thing y' ever saw."

Mark proceeded to his son's side and said, "I've got to get back to work."

"Are we not getting a real Christmas tree, Dad? Pop says we could go out to Cus'n Jem's and cut one."

Just once, Mark wished that someone would be satisfied with his efforts. Just once. "*Cousin* Jem. Not cus'n. And we're not going out to his place to cut anything." His sigh was audible and puzzled. "Don't you like this, Spence? Leicester's an important new artist. And this is *his* conception of what a Christmas tree should look like."

Spencer was less than impressed. "I think the guy's a dork. It's got mold on it. Did you have to get it because Grandfather Constance said to? Because he liked it?"

Mark shifted his weight, uncomfortable with a statement that, despite its tone of disrespect, was just perhaps too close to the truth. But leave it to Spencer. He was always asking penetrating questions, embarrassingly pertinent, unsettling in that they so often had no easy answers.

But how could he expect the boy to understand? Abel Constance was more than Mark's boss. More than Spencer's grandfather. He was Mark's former father-in-law. He was Mark's mentor. He was the one person who had helped Mark climb down from the hills and into the twentieth century. Into a world with indoor plumbing, for God's sake. Abel had offered

Mark the opportunity to leave the past behind forever. He dangled the carrot, and Mark sprinted around and around the track.

Yes, Abel had liked the sculpture. And yes, he had suggested that Mark get one for the house.

Mark contemplated the expensive bronze tree before him. Abel certainly wasn't the only reason Mark had bought the sculpture. After all, the artist had renown. Ownership signified membership. Distinction. Class. It irritated him that Spencer and Pop couldn't see that. Stealing a glance at his father, who was fingering the sculpture like a small child, Mark felt uncommonly tired. Pop's shirt was half untucked from pants that were baggy and threadbare. And he had the audacity to wear an apricot-colored, silk handkerchief in his left breast pocket, as if that camouflaged who he was and where he had come from. Mark grimaced. As usual, Pop had forgotten to shave this morning, and oh, good grief, his fly was undone again.

Mark straightened the tie beneath his Hickey Freeman vest and coat. "I've got to get back to the office." He fished in the inside jacket pocket for his money clip, then peeled off a few crisp bills for his son. "Here, go buy yourself a new toy at the mall this afternoon."

Spencer took the proffered money, but glared at it. "You promised to take me to Santa's Village," he whined.

Fatigue settled over Mark and, like a dust-laden rug, weighted him down. "I forgot, Spence. I—that is, Abel and I are entertaining some clients here tonight. It's something I've got to do."

A curtain dropped over the boy's face. "Oh. Well, sure, then, that's okay."

Failing to shove aside the ever-present guilt, Mark said, "Maybe you and Pop could go together to Santa's Village. That would be fun, wouldn't it?"

"Sure," said Spencer, walking over to his grandfather. "We'll have a great time. Hey, Pop, your barn door's open."

Pop looked down at his pants. "Well, I'll be dipped. I thought I felt a draft."

After zipping up, Pop finally lit up his cigar and grinned down at his favorite person. "Boy, I think we ought to go whup up somethin' to eat, want t'?"

"Potato-chip sandwich?"

Pop grinned around his cigar. "With tons of mayonnaise."

Mark watched the two of them stroll arm in arm toward the kitchen, totally compatible, totally at ease with one another. No gaps or chasms that had to be bridged. Friends.

His father's voice droned repetitively, echoing through the undecked halls of what Mark liked to refer to as tasteful minimalist decor.

"Now pine," Pop was telling Spencer, "that there's a Christmas tree. 'Course, there's nothing nobler than a Douglas fir, but they don't grow in our parts. Always cottoned to the smell of cedar, though. Cut me a cedar back when yore daddy was about yore age. Big, fat thing. Ellie shore did love that tree. Think that was yore granny's all-time favorite..."

Mark, fighting the subconscious urge to remember the sweet-smelling ghosts of Christmases past, planned a counterattack. He would put off going to work just for a few minutes. There was something he had to do first. Something he had to say to Pop, and he might as well get it over with before he lost the courage.

"Pop?"

He had put it off long enough. "Could you two wait on your snack? I need to talk to you."

They stopped and looked back. Mark shifted nervously.

"Why, shore, sonny. Listen, Spenner boy, you go on in and start getting the tater chips out. I'll be 'long directly." Pop looked for a place to stub out his cigar. He knew Mark didn't like the smell, and something told him right now was not the time to aggravate. Finding no ashtray, he opened the front door and flicked it onto the ice-coated lawn. Snow rarely made it to Bolton County, just ice, usually, and, in the past few years, even that was a rarity. Before his sister Cora died, she claimed she'd read somewheres that the earth was getting hotter every year. "Heatin' up like a Franklin stove," she said.

"Gonna melt the polar ice caps, and we're gonna all wash away." Cora tried to get her husband, Ronnie, to build them an ark, but Ronnie never could work up the enthusiasm.

Pop stared out over the icy sheen and thought about his sisters, Cora and Irma Lee, and his baby brother, Skeeter. "All gone now," he said with a shake of his head as he closed the door. He glanced across the room and, in the brief moment before rejoining the present, was surprised to see Mark standing there. Why, the boy was plum grown.

"Here, Pop, let's sit down for a minute."

Mark arranged himself at one end of the white couch, and Pop came over and sat at the other end, each of them angled so that they faced one another. Mark draped his arm along the back of the sofa and crossed an ankle over his knee. He hoped he looked more relaxed than he felt.

Pop beheld his son, dressed as always in a crisp, three-piece suit, and thought he looked as tense as a rabbit cornered in a smoking log. But then, Mark always looked tense. A handsome boy, though. Looked like his mama, with all that dark, shiny hair and those questioning blue eyes. Smart, too. Don't know where he got that, though. Sure wasn't from his old man. Ellie was always telling Pop he didn't have the sense of a plucked chicken in a downpour. But Mark, well, that boy came home every time with straight As on his report card. Actually seemed to like school, too.

When all the other boys were quitting to stay home and help their daddies bale hay or even to help those geologists take plugs from the ground before they decided there wasn't enough oil under there to mess with, Mark had flat-out refused. He was bound and determined to go to school. Got too smart for Miss Bill's classroom, so he had to take the bus into Edgeton every day. In high school, he was elected president of the honor society, then voted the most likely to succeed. He got himself a scholarship to college.

"I shore am proud of y', son," said Pop, beaming at his grown-up boy.

Mark cleared the lump from his throat and suddenly wished he'd gone to work, wished he was anywhere but facing his father. Heart-to-hearts weren't his thing. But the time was now. Before he completely chickened out, he had to forge ahead. "I don't know quite where to begin."

"Look, son, if it's about that tree."

"Tree?"

Pop pointed to the bronze sculpture.

"Oh," said Mark. "No, it's not about the tree. It's about Spence."

"That boy's gonna be as tall as a poplar, I reckon. Jest like you. But he's got his mama's mouth, don't he?" Pop scowled at that. "Got more sense'n her, though. Any woman that'd leave her young 'un and run off with some fella to New Mexico, never could understand what y' saw in—"

"You know I don't want to talk about Angela, Dad. That's over, okay?"

Pop pursed his lips and nodded slowly. "Shore, sonny, whatever y' say."

"I got a letter from the school, Pop. About Spencer. They are hoping that his behavior will improve over the holiday. They're demanding, actually."

"Shoo," murmured Pop. "Buncha old squawkin' hens who want nothin' but creosoted fence posts lined up behind them desks. Y' should put him in the public school down the street, son. It looks like a dandy school."

"We've talked about this before, Pop. He stays at Parkhill."

Pop shrugged, then pulled out his clippers and went to work on his nails. Mark saw the clippings drop to his lap, then watched his father pick them up one by one and make a pile on the coffee table.

"It would help if you didn't keep Spencer up so late at night." Mark hoped he was listening. The nail clippings kept piling up. "You two are always banging around in the kitchen at midnight, making those fried-egg sandwiches or whatever. And drinking Cokes. It's not good for him."

"Just havin' us a bit of a healthy snack, son. Now I know some folks say you shouldn't eat late at night, but I never cottoned to that opinion myself. I figure that—''

"Pop?"

"Yes, son? Oh, did I 't'rupt y'?"

"Midnight is past Spencer's bedtime. You've got to stop keeping him up so late. He needs his sleep. And I need my sleep, which I can't possibly get with you two banging around down here in the middle of the night."

"You're right, son. I got to work on the noise level. I figure an eight-year-old's noise level is about equal to—''

"Pop?"

"Hm?"

"There are a couple of other things. A couple of problems we need to talk over."

Pop patted his shirt pockets until he remembered that he'd tossed out the cigar. He wished he had one to chew on, at least.

"Clara spoke to me today."

"Fine housekeeper, Mark. Fine girl. I been teaching her how to make a bed proper. I think y' ought to give her a raise."

To Mark's relief, the nail clipper was put away. "She told me that you took down all the drapes in the dining room and tried to stuff them in the washing machine."

"They looked a mite dingy. I thought they could use some bluin'."

Mark closed his eyes. Clara had caught them in time. Caught Pop right in the act, but before any actual damage was done. "She said she had to spend half a day putting them back up and getting the wrinkles out. We have a dry-cleaning service that does that, you know. You don't need to be worrying with it."

"Oh, well, I just thought that—"

"And Manuel had to replant the flower bed. He said you watered the pansies so much, they floated right out of the bed, along with all the mulch."

"The problem is root structure," said Pop. "Them high-fallutin' nursery starts don't have the root structure they should. Now, yore mama used to have the pertiest flowers I ever did—"

"And these incidences with Spencer," Mark continued, undaunted. "He gets in enough trouble at school. But it's nothing compared to when he's with you."

"Well, now, a little moon pie or egg sandwich late at night don't seem so bad."

"Jack Lawrence called me at work this morning."

Pop's response was a blank look.

"You remember, our next-door neighbor?"

"Oh. That Lawrence."

"Yes, that one."

"Well, I reckon he's a mite piqued about that dog situation, right?"

Mark sighed. "What on earth were you and Spencer thinking?"

"Spenner thought the dog looked lonesome. He didn't have a collar or tag, so we thought we'd keep him around till we could put an ad in the paper."

"So you put him in the Lawrences' backyard."

"They got a dog. We figured them two could play together."

"They have a French poodle, Pop. A grand champion."

"Never did like that breed, myself. I always liked a good bird dog. Useful breed, bird dogs, and—"

"The Lawrences' poodle also happens to be in heat."

Pop sucked at his bridge of false teeth. "Well, I'll be dipped."

"Have you ever seen a cross between a bulldog and a poodle, Pop?"

"Not a perty sight, I reckon."

"No," said Mark. "Not pretty." He massaged the back of his neck. Maybe this could have all been said later. It didn't *have* to be done right now. There was always tomorrow.

"I've been thinking about something, Pop. Something that you might want to consider." He reached into his coat pocket and pulled out a full-color brochure. He handed it over to his father.

Pop patted his shirt for glasses, then remembered he had stepped on them this morning. He squinted his eyes and played trombone with the pamphlet until it came into focus. But it was a gesture meant only to save face. They both knew he couldn't read.

"Windward Retirement Estates." Mark pointed to the words for his father.

Pop squinted at his son, then back at the brochure while Mark continued to read and point. "'Fully planned community for the golden years.'"

Mark retreated to his corner of the couch. "Just something to think about."

"Well, now." Pop stared at the brochure for a long time, pretending to read, perusing each color photo. "I reckon I'm happy right where I am, son. Right here with you and Spenner Jake."

"I know you are, Pop. I just thought that—I mean, it's not that we don't want you around—I certainly don't want you to think that. No, sir. It's just that— well, I thought you might be happier with people your own age. You know, people who have your same— well, interests."

"If y' need more space here, I could go back and live with Cus'n Cooter, or in with Matty Rae."

Pop had come out of his corner with both gloves on, and Mark reeled from the blow. "It's not a matter of space. And you know I've got money. You don't have to live back there. This Windward place is nice, Dad. Real posh."

"What'd I want with posh?"

Mark scanned the large white living room. His gaze scouted out all the expensive things he had worked so hard to obtain. Paintings and art objects and rare books. Was he the only one who saw them? Who appreciated them?

Pop studied the brochure for what was to Mark an agonizingly long time. Silence ticked by like a clock that needed rewinding. The brochure fluttered from his father's fingers and landed in his lap. Looking much older than he had only moments before, Pop picked up the brochure, as if it were tainted, and handed it to Mark. He cranked himself up from the couch.

"Guess I'd best be getting this old body out to the kitchen. Promised Spenner a tater-chip sandwich." He didn't look at his son, and each ponderous syllable fell like an indictment against Mark's ears.

He sat for several minutes after Pop had gone into the kitchen. When he finally stood and reached for his overcoat, draped over the crewelwork wingback chair, he knew he, too, in the past few minutes, had aged. He wrestled his arms into the coat sleeves and wondered why he felt so bad about the conversation. It wasn't a *bad* idea. Abel had handed him the brochure a week ago. Mark had carried it around, waiting for the right moment, the idea growing more vivid in his mind each day.

A retirement home was a solution. Pop could be with friends his own age. Spencer could get his life on track and learn some discipline for a change. Clara and Manuel would be relieved. And Mark wouldn't have to listen to the incessant ramblings and unwanted advice from his father. It made great sense, this idea did. So why did he now feel as if there was a granite boulder lodged in the center of his chest?

He opened the front door and stepped outside. The thin layer of ice had coated the front walk, and the bottoms of his new shoes were as slick as Teflon. It was an effort to negotiate the driveway. He opened the door of his BMW and situated himself behind the wheel. He was just inserting his key into the ignition when he noticed an indignant eight-year-old standing without a coat or hat beside the car.

He rolled down his window. "Get back inside, Spence, before you freeze. I'll see you tonight."

"No, you won't. You're going to be entertaining tonight."

"I'll come in and tuck you in when I get home."

"I'll be asleep already."

Cloud vapors spilled in staccato notes from his lungs. "I've got to go, son. I'll see you tonight."

Spencer's mouth was drawn into a tight, thin arc. He tried unsuccessfully to cram his fists into the front pockets of his jeans. "I don't want Pop to go."

Mark cursed his bad timing. "What were you doing, listening at the kitchen door?"

"Yes, and I think you're mean."

Nothing was going right today. The earth's tilt was all wrong. And that conversation with Pop had disaster written all over it. Over the past week Mark had worked and reworked the dialogue in his head. He had planned it out so well, but it just hadn't come out right at all. Pop had been hurt. Mark had seen that right off. And now Spencer had heard the whole damn thing and was throwing a tantrum.

"You can't make Pop go," he whined. "If he goes, I'm going."

Mark was tired and frustrated and under too much pressure from all sides. He wasn't in the mood to take any flak from an eight-year-old. "It's none of your concern," he snapped, then immediately regretted the remark. "Look, I'm going to work, Spencer. I've got a busy afternoon. You go have a good time with Pop."

Several minutes later he was still sitting in the driveway, staring at the closed door to his house, the one Spencer had slammed shut.

Mark wasn't normally one to wallow in self-pity but, for the moment, he felt justified. When did the struggle ever end? When would he ever reach a plateau when life's wrinkles smoothed out? Too many people depended on him. Too many people needed him. He felt pulled in a hundred different directions. So much was expected of him. And to top it off, he never could completely escape the life into which he had been born.

He had done everything in his power to leave behind the boy who had grown up on the side of Blue Mountain, along the muddy waters of Lindy Creek. That skinny, barefoot sprig who had lived in a tiny unpainted house with washboard siding, with a worn springy sofa on the front porch and a hand-pump well and a big washtub in the front yard was not him. That boy was gone forever. In his place was a man of substance and wealth, a man who had found success in his career and whose class transition had been smooth and inevitable. He had graduated from college with honors. He had hired on with one of the best aeronautical engineering firms in the country. He had married the boss's daughter. Together they had bred the perfect blond-haired, blue-eyed child. He had a big house in an acceptable suburb. He had done all that was necessary to create for himself a new life, a new identity.

So when had everything gone haywire?

Angela had left him. Spencer was into trouble at school more than he was out. Pop had moved in and, ever since, had consistently chipped away at the crust of prosperity Mark had carefully constructed for himself. At the same time, Abel Constance was pushing Mark to reach for even bigger and better things.

Too many expectations.

And now both Pop and Spencer were mad at him.

It wasn't as if he was talking about throwing Pop out into the streets. Why, Windward Retirement Estates would cost as much a month as the mortgage payment on this house. Pop had been living with them for almost a year now. And he'd gotten used to the finer things in life. Hadn't he? He had a big bedroom all to himself with his own television and bathroom. No more trips in the middle of a cold night out to the loo. No more fighting a frozen well pump for water to boil on the stove.

No way was Mark going to let his father go back to the mountain and live with Cousin Cooter or with Matty Rae and her sot of a husband. If Windward didn't suit Pop's fancy, then Mark would just find something else that would.

But something had to be done. He intended to start the new year off right. Marching onward, never looking back.

Pumped up with a new sense of purpose, and looking ahead instead of behind, Mark started the BMW, backed out of the drive and skated like a wet cake of soap into the chrome grille of an oncoming Mercedes.

Another wrinkle.

Chapter Two

The town had started out as Edge Town, then became Edgeville, and finally the city council settled on Edgeton. The founding fathers started with a few brick factories and wood bungalows that they built right at the base of the rolling hills. Now, forty years later, the town had oozed like algae down and over the swampland to the west.

In the cramped, washed-out district where Edgeton had first begun its commercial rise, and which was now slowly and somewhat agonizingly being transformed into a neighborhood, Leah Johnson sat on the piano bench in her renovated bungalow. Beside her was a tone-deaf girl of ten, whose short, stubby fingers were now desecrating the once lovely "O Holy Night."

Outside, the thin layer of ice gave the area buildings and streets a liquid sheen. A world frozen in place.

"That's very good," Leah said with admirable enthusiasm, when the girl stopped playing. "Now, let's try it from here again. This is in adagio. Slow it down just a bit through here."

With great gusto, the child banged her way through the next fifteen minutes, while Leah's concentration drifted time and time again to the ice-draped world outside her window. Inside, she was warm and snug, her small house heated adequately by a wood-burning stove that sat proudly in the corner. In the summers, its belly housed sprigs of baby's breath. But now it grumbled contentedly with fat pine logs that Dill Moody had brought into the DeHaven Center for her. Leah hadn't been working the day he'd come in, but he'd left them with Lilla DeHaven, the owner. Dill lived about ten miles back in the hills and came to town only on rare and very special occasions, always walking the entire distance. It made Leah feel good to think she had been special enough for him to make the trip. He had brought the logs those ten miles in a wheelbarrow.

A log cracked and sizzled in the grate. The two cats, Gopher and Brenda, were curled up together on the sofa, asleep. Leah loved her house, but never so much as on chill winter days. She felt insulated and at peace. Her own house, her own self-sufficiency. Independence. A burden to no one.

The living room where she conducted her piano lessons was not large, but she had managed to cram it full of all the things she loved so much. Cluttering the wood shelves that lined one wall were photographs of friends, old and new, along with hundreds of crafts handmade by Blue Mountain folks who lived among the hills. At most times of the year, dried flowers decorated the top of the television, the windowsills and the wood coffee table. But now every available surface was taken up with Christmas decorations. Leah had grapevine wreaths hung on the walls and handmade candles on the table. A sprig of fresh mistletoe hung from the light in the center of the room. Holly and pine boughs were draped in doorways and on the top of the pine bureau. A carved nutcracker stood guard on the television, and countless stuffed Santas and mice and snowmen took up the few spots that remained.

Leah glanced around the room and felt soothed. Everything was in place. There were no vacancies, no empty spaces. Nothing left incomplete.

She patiently gave the necessary directions to her pupil and forced herself not to cringe every time the girl hit the wrong note, until the girl's mother, bless her soul, arrived to whisk her away.

Alone after a full morning of lessons, Leah flipped on the tape deck. The Christmas sounds of the Mormon Tabernacle Choir spilled into the room, enhanced by the aroma of cinnamon and apple spice that simmered on the back of the stove, and framed by the jumble of colorful and textured decorations that filled the small house.

For some people, it would have been tempting to plop down on the sofa and spend the afternoon listening to music, hypnotized by the icy drizzle and just letting the afternoon unwind. For some people. But not for Leah Johnson. She was just gearing up.

After eating a quick sandwich, she cooked up a batch of fudge and spread it in a buttered pan. Then, from the closet, she pulled down a large carton filled with mittens. These mittens, earmarked for the homeless, represented the first project for SHARE, the organization she had recently formed and of which she was, so far, the only member.

Leah slipped on her coat but didn't bother with her gloves and hat. She wasn't going that far. Lugging the cumbersome carton of mittens with her, she left the house, taking great care not to slip on the icy stoop. Once on the sidewalk, she shifted the weight of the carton to her hip and walked the fifteen feet to the door of the DeHaven Center. Her house was attached to the large renovated warehouse, and the headboard of her bed rested opposite the center's wall of second- or third-hand shoes and purses.

The store smelled of floor wax and freshly laundered clothes. Lilla DeHaven believed in running a clean ship, just as her mother had before her. Country born and bred, she took great pride in her endowment. The floor glistened with a spit-polished shine, and the almost endless rows of hand-me-down clothes were stacked with military precision. Underwear was folded in six-inch squares; hats were lined up according to head size. Shoes were set on racks with the toes pointing all in the same direction. Many a hapless volunteer had received a tongue-lashing from Lilla when things were not aligned just so. And browsers who thought they could rummage through the clothes then leave the messy stacks behind were in for a big surprise. If some aimless drifter wandered in looking for a warm berth, Lilla would flap her arms and her big apron as if she were shooing brooding hens out of the roost. She took her work most seriously.

Leah's house reflected a lack of desire for such order, but when she was working at the center she stacked and aligned and swept and dusted just the way Lilla demanded it be done.

On this cold afternoon the store felt warm and welcoming to Leah. She carried the box of mittens to the back storeroom, and placed them in the corner where Lilla wouldn't have to trip over them.

"Y' sure y' don't need help with those?" asked Lilla when Leah came out of the storeroom.

"No, I'll be fine. I'm going to start tomorrow after my morning piano lessons. Can you believe it, I was able to collect fifty-three pairs!"

"My lands," said Lilla. "Think of that." She was realigning and alphabetizing the used books on what she referred to as "the library table," and Leah hurried over to help her. The bell above the door tinkled, signaling customers. A couple came in and quickly closed out the frosty day behind them. With bony fingers, the man drew his wet battered hat down to his chest, and the haggard-looking woman at his side, bulging with pregnancy, looked around shyly. They both stood hesitant inside the door.

Lilla DeHaven took care of that. "Come on in." She beamed at her customers. "Glad to have y'. I tell y' what, that ice out there is downright awful, ain't it?"

"Yes'm," said the man, venturing a step forward.

"What can I help y' good folks with today?"

The woman was glancing around as if she'd never seen such a rich display of goods. The man fingered his hat and said, "We come for some things for a new one. My wife here's having us a new one right soon."

"Well, I see that," said Lilla. She marched over to the woman, draped a proprietary arm around her shoulder and led her straight to the aisle of baby clothes. They were laid out according to age and size on eight different folding tables. Leah had spent all afternoon yesterday matching up the tiny outfits. She knew Lilla could be proud of her display.

"It ain't our first," said the woman. "We've got four others."

"But y' want somethin' new for this 'un, right?"

The woman smiled shyly.

"Well, let me help y' pick out what y' need."

Leah walked up to the man, who was still hovering anxiously by the door. "Can I give you a cup of coffee?"

He seemed hesitant to accept any handout at all, but he followed Leah to a far corner of the store where a table held a coffeepot and cut squares of fresh-baked cake. She poured him a cup and picked up the plate. He took the coffee, but hesitated over the cake.

Even from where she stood across the store, Lilla didn't miss his hesitation. "That there's my Russian Communist tea cake," she boomed authoritatively. "Y' gotta try it. It's so good it'll make your tongue slap your jaw teeth out."

The man jumped when Lilla hollered, and quickly grabbed a piece. He didn't know how to go about refusing Russian Communist cake, and nobody refused Lilla DeHaven.

It was a typically slow winter afternoon at the DeHaven Center but, after the couple had gone, it gave Lilla and Leah a chance to talk and to sort through some boxes of clothes that had been delivered yesterday afternoon.

"That woman's probably got more young 'uns than she knows what to do with, and she probably has trouble feeding 'em enough. But I betcha each one of 'em is real special t' her."

"You're probably right," said Leah, contrasting the image with the reality of her own family. She had been the only child, born into the lap of luxury. But special? She had never been that to her parents. She had been a burden.

Lilla stole a glance at her young co-worker. Leah Johnson was such a pretty thing, colorful as a day-lily, but soft and loving like a velvety pansy in winter. There was a sadness about her, too, an indefinable kind of thing that Lilla couldn't quite put her finger on. She was always so busy going and doing and fixing, but it was always for other people. Lilla couldn't help but think the girl would be a fine catch for any man. But somehow, she didn't much think Leah was looking for that sort of thing right now. She kind of thought Leah could use some fixing herself.

Leah stayed and helped until five, then ran home for a quick bite of supper before heading off to help with the youth meeting at the church.

She hadn't always been so outwardly directed. There had been a time, and not so very long ago, when she had lived solely for herself, when life had been meant to party away, when days and nights had blended in a happy-go-lucky haze of endless self-indulgence.

The daughter of the paper-towel king, Winslow Johnson, she had grown up with all the trappings that money could buy. Everyone had said her father was a busy man, and she supposed that was why he never had much time to spend with her. Her mother had no time for her, either, but that was because she was absorbed with more pressing societal matters. A child, to Eva Johnson, was really nothing more than an irritating nuisance. A dress-up doll that didn't know when to stay on the shelf.

It was childish to have railed against that emotional neglect, but that was exactly what Leah had done. Rather than opt for choices that might ingratiate her to her mother's circle of friends or with her father's business, she had deliberately set off to pursue her own reckless life-style. Allowed to go her own way, she managed to eke out a college degree in music education. But she certainly had no intention of working. Ever. What would be the point? She had all the money she needed.

From the time she had learned that she would not get the love she so desperately wanted from her parents, she had turned to others. Innocent and unwitting, she became a pawn for men who sought her money or her connections. She was promised the moon. Time and time again. She longed for love, but what she got were empty promises and enough heartbreak to last a lifetime.

She no longer looked for love.

For a couple of years after college, she made the circuit of friends' parties in the States and abroad. She collected dozens of traffic tickets for driving her Mercedes too fast. She drank the finest champagnes to excess. Like a long, tumultuous slide down a rocky slope, Leah's life was tumbling at breakneck speed. But she didn't see until it was almost too late.

When she thought of it now, it seemed a long time ago. And it was as if she had been living inside another woman's skin. She still had the same energy and enthusiasm that she always had, but now, instead of being directed toward self-destruction, it was directed toward helping others. If she could save herself, she figured, she could save the rest of the world, too. Besides, as long as people needed her, she could never be a burden on anyone again. And as long as life was filled with the needs of others, she would never have to worry about her own needs. Staying busy, that was the key. Never an empty moment, a vacant space.

So Leah didn't know the meaning of the word unwind. What with all there was to do and with so many people out there to organize and fix, she had to stay in perpetual overdrive just to cover the distance.

And she still had miles to go.

CLAD IN STRIPED PAJAMAS, with a stuffed purple-eyed monster perched in his lap, Spencer nested in the middle of Pop's rumpled bedcovers and watched him pack. Mark had left for work hours ago, and Spencer and Pop had made a commotion in the kitchen fixing blueberry waffles. Clara, who was left to clean up the mess, had sent them off with a stern scowl and a string of Spanish epithets that fortunately they could not translate.

Spencer watched Pop move around the cluttered quarters. Pop's room was in direct contrast with the rest of the house. Clothes were strewn about. A pair of socks was hung to dry from a makeshift clothesline draped between two chairs. A photo album, its pictures yellowing beneath crisp plastic, lay open beside the bed. A handmade cane, carved from cypress wood, was propped against the window. Pop didn't need it for walking but it was an age-old friend, and he never left the house without it.

"I don't want you to go, Pop."

"Well, sonny boy, I got my matilda all packed up here, and I'm ready to travel."

"I want to go with you," begged Spencer. "I don't want to stay here."

"Well, sakes alive. What do y' think Herbert'd say if you just up and left him?"

Spencer thought about that, then said, "Hamsters don't talk, Grandpa."

"Well, he can think, cain't he?"

"I s'pose."

"And he'd miss y', right?"

"I s'pose. But I'm going to miss you."

Pop busied himself with the zipper of his haversack so he wouldn't have to face his grandson. When he realized he could avoid it no longer, he looked and saw that the boy's blue eyes glistened with tears. One wayward strand of blond hair drooped over his pale forehead. Pop felt something wet and painful behind his own eyes, but he guessed a clean break was best for all.

"It's jest that time, Spenner boy. Time for Pop to move on. There ain't no way in h—" He cleared his throat. "No way I'm gonna be locked away in some home with a bunch of ol' toothless geezers who wouldn't know a good time if it spit 'em smack dab in the face. No, sirree."

"Are you gonna go live with Cousin Cooter?"

Pop closed the photo album and set it on the dresser. "Nah. Think I'd like to get to know this ol' town. Been meaning to for a long time, y' know."

"But you've lived around here all your life."

"Yeah, but I lived on the mountain, y' see. Came to town occasional, but only to sell somethin' or buy somethin'. Never spent time here, y' see. Lived on the mountain all my life, till yore dad ast me to come stay with you and him."

"But where will you stay now?"

Pop grabbed the socks from the line strung between the chairs. He set the bag on the bed, unzipped it and stuffed the socks inside. "Oh, I reckon I'll find me a bridge somewheres. Set me up a cardboard box 'neath it. That'll do me just fine."

"Don't you want some money? Daddy has lots of money. You could take some with you."

"What in tarnation would I do with money, sonny boy?" Pop zipped the bag again. "I ain't never had more'n twenty dollars in my pocket at a time. Money don't mean nothin' to me."

"Daddy likes money. He's always working so he can get more. He says you've got to have money to live right."

"Well, some folks put more store in it than others."

"How come Daddy does, if you don't?"

Pop sat on the edge of the rumpled bed, and his eyes skirted from Spencer to the stuffed monster to the packed bag and back. "When your daddy was just a little older'n you, he started comin' to town to school. He saw how all them other kids lived." Pop plucked absently at the bed covers. "Y' see, Spenner, I think they was kinda hard on your daddy. Said things to him, y' know. He never talked 'bout it much, but I think it did somethin' to his way of thinking."

Spencer felt as if he was going to cry, but he didn't want to in front of his grandfather. Still, he didn't want Pop to go. "I could come with you, Grandpa," he pleaded. "I could live under the bridge, too. That would be neat, wouldn't it?"

Pop stiffened his spine. "Nope," he said, standing up and reaching for his bag. "Goin' on my own, sonny boy." He forced a skip into his step. "Got to stay on my toes."

"How will I find you, if you go?"

"Oh, I'll send word to y' and tell y' what bridge I'm living under. Y' can drop by for a game of crazy eights now and then."

"Why is Daddy so mean!" cried Spencer, walloping his monster doll on the head.

Pop stood near the bed, taking stock of his grandson and of the facts of life. "Yore daddy's not mean, son. He's a fine man."

"He doesn't care about us. He wants to put you in some old people's home and he doesn't do anything with me. All he cares about is that stupid work of his."

"He's a busy man, Spenner. He's trying to give y' a good life. It ain't easy for him being on his own, but he cares about y' a bunch."

"Ever since Mommy left us, he doesn't want me."

"That ain't true, sonny. Don't y' never think that. It's been mighty hard for him the last couple of years, that's all."

"All he does is work." Spencer pressed his face into the doll's green yarn hair. "When Daddy was my age, did you work all the time the way he does?"

"No, but then we didn't have nothin' to show for it, neither. Mark, well, he just wants somethin' more out of life, I guess. He wants to give y' more'n I was able to give him."

"Like what?"

The transition in perspective from cardboard boxes under a bridge to more material matters was quite a leap, but Pop gave it a try. "Well, Mark had to pay for his own schoolin'. He had to work for a car and for just 'bout everything he ever had. He didn't have all the toys and things that y' got."

Spencer hit the monster again. "I just want him to spend more time with me. I don't care about all that other stuff." He pulled the doll against his chest and said gently, "I wish I had a mom and dad like everybody else has."

Pop stepped close and rested his hand on top of Spencer's head. "I know y' do, sonny boy. I know y' do."

Spencer stood on the bed and threw his arms around Pop's neck. Grandfather and grandson leaned into each other, finding in each other's arms the home and the love they both so desperately needed.

"G'bye, sonny boy." Pop disengaged himself and stepped toward the door, his pack in one hand, his cane in the other.

With tears in his eyes, Spencer watched his grandfather leave the room. He stood rooted to the spot in the center of the unmade bed as footsteps and cane tip clumped down the stairs and through the foyer. The front door opened and closed with a finality that pierced the heart. "Bye, Grandpa," he whispered sadly, while he crushed his stuffed friend against his body.

Pop was his best friend in the whole world. Christmas wouldn't be worth having without him.

Seconds slipped by, then, suddenly, the monster fell to the bed covers. Making a snap decision, Spencer jumped to the floor, dashed down the long hallway to his room, grabbed two mismatched sneakers from beneath the bed and crammed them on his feet, not bothering to tie them.

Bounding down the stairs, he threw open the door and ran out into the cold December afternoon, racing down the sidewalk in the only direction Pop could possibly have gone.

Chapter Three

With an empty cardboard carton and a heart full of commitment to everything but self, Leah walked down Second and turned the corner at Ridgeway. The town was laid out in a latticework grid that offered little rhyme or reason for the naming of streets. Third, of course, followed Second, and Fourth followed Third, but after that, Ridgeway turned into Elm as it crossed Maxwell. Her bungalow and the DeHaven Center were on the corner of Elm and Maxwell.

Leah had lived in this old section of the city for three years now, and she figured she could find her way through the maze of streets blindfolded. She had started out here with Vista, and when her commitment to the program had ended, she had decided to stay on.

The sky was heavy with moisture, a sullen gray that covered three-quarters of the sky. Only in the west was there a hint of blue, but even there the sun was rapidly disappearing behind the jagged line of gray buildings.

Christmas smells pervaded the cold air, drifting in from everywhere, from the corner stand where a man sold hot apple cider, from the vacant lot across the street where Mr. Samuels was selling scrawny Christmas trees. A Salvation Army bell clanged repetitively in the distance, and red tinsel bells swayed from the traffic lights in the intersections. The atmosphere was charged with expectancy.

Leah's pace quickened in anticipation of home. It was nice to have her own warm, secure place to go home to. She had spent the afternoon handing out mittens to people who had nowhere at all to go. The temperature was expected to drop to a record low tonight, and the already burdened shelters and missions were hard-pressed to handle everyone. For some, doorways and narrow alleys would have to suffice.

The sky and the earth converged, leaving no line of demarcation. The air became a liquid screen, crystallized and bitterly cold. She watched a young man with long greasy hair and a long greasy beard, a crutch wedged under one arm and a bottle of liquor gripped in his hand, lumber aimlessly down the sidewalk, heading nowhere in particular, accumulating seconds of the nothings and nowheres that made up his life.

For people like that, Leah knew, there was no anticipation for the coming of Christmas. For them, hope had lost all meaning.

Many of her Vista co-workers had given up trying to find redress. They could not cure all the ailments society had inflicted upon itself, and they had readily admitted defeat. Inequities were part and parcel of life. But Leah refused to admit defeat. She had no limitations. Her energy was boundless, her determination formidable.

When she compared her life now to her old life, she felt fulfilled. She loved her job as music director of the church. She enjoyed instructing young children on the piano. She took great pride in the house on Maxwell that she had renovated. She had friends and goals and independence, and she needed no one. Too many years of desperately needing her parents' love and attention—a need that had gone unfulfilled—had caused her to carve out a niche for herself alone, and never to need anyone so desperately again.

She pulled up the collar on her navy wool jacket and shoved her hands into her pockets. Only a few more blocks and she would be home. She could throw some logs in the potbellied stove and turn on some Christmas music. Maybe she would heat up some of the vegetable soup she had made this morning.

She was only two blocks from home when she saw him. A small, forlorn figure, huddled on a hard wooden bench in the small park, his arms folded across his body and his chin tucked against his chest. A thick mass of pale blond hair swirled madly in the cold evening breeze. The park, except for the boy, was empty.

She waited for the traffic to clear, then she crossed the street.

"What are you doing out here in the cold all by yourself?"

Spencer gravely studied her heavy camouflage boots before lifting his chin and giving her a suspicious once-over. "I'm not supposed to talk to strangers."

Leah never thought of herself as a stranger. She was a friend to all. This was a new experience. "That's good advice. I just thought maybe you were lost."

"Nah. Not me. My grandpa is."

She retreated deeper inside her coat. "Your grandpa?"

"Yeah, I'm waiting for him."

"I see." The gray gloom settled around her. She checked out the small park, but saw no one else. "Is he nearby?"

The boy shrugged, then pointed to the bar across the street. "He might be in there."

Leah read the tacky neon sign that hung by two thin wires above the door. She looked at the boy. "Does he go in there often?"

"His name's Pop."

She glanced at the sign again. It read Pop's Place. "Oh, he owns the bar?"

The boy shook his head. "Nah. But his name's Pop."

"I see. And you think he might be in there?"

The boy nodded and shivered. "Yeah, but he doesn't go to places like that. I mean, at home he keeps his bottle in the pantry closet. He thinks I don't know, but I do. He won't keep it with my dad's stuff. My dad has a bar with mirrors and glass shelves and all that stuff, but Pop won't keep his bottle there. He keeps it in the pantry, and every night before dinner he goes into the pantry and closes the door. I watch the clock and it's fifteen minutes exactly. Then he comes out. His cheeks are always kinda red, and he always gives me a little pat right here on my shoulder."

Leah smiled at the blond-haired waif. He had been instructed not to talk to strangers, yet she felt as if they were already old buddies. She glanced down at his mismatched sneakers. When he shivered again, she set down the empty carton, unbuttoned her heavy wool coat and slipped it off. Trying to ignore the cold that bit with sharp teeth through her sweatshirt and jeans, she draped the coat around his shoulders. "I know that I'm a stranger," she said, "but I'm a little bit concerned about you. Would you like for me to see if your grandfather is in there?"

He pulled the coat around him and snuggled inside. "Yeah. They wouldn't let me in. This big ugly guy at the door told me to go away. But don't be scared of him. He's just a big jerk."

Leah grinned. "Okay, I won't be scared." She squared her shoulders in preparation for battle. "You just wait right here, okay? What's your grandfather's full name?"

"Pop Carruthers."

Leah crossed the busy street and walked up to the bar. The big ugly jerk appraised her, but she didn't cower under his stare. There was very little in life that could frighten Leah Johnson away.

Inside, the bar smelled of cheap liquor and sweat. Old sweat. The place was almost empty. There were only a bartender and two patrons, both young. Along the mirror behind the counter draped a twisted strand of red and gold tinsel. "Grandma Got Run Over by a Reindeer" played on the jukebox. It didn't take long for Leah to realize that the boy's grandfather was not in there. This was not the kind of place for a man who drank in a pantry closet. "Merry Christmas," she said to the bouncer on her way out.

She hurried across the street and knelt in front of the boy. "I'm afraid he's not in there."

He looked as if he were about to cry. "He's lost, I'll bet. I just know he is."

"Oh, I'm sure he can find his way home."

He shook his head. "He isn't coming home. He ran away."

Leah rubbed her hands along the arms of her sweatshirt. "Why would he want to do that?"

"My dad wanted him to move out. He wanted him to go to one of those places where old people live. Pop didn't want to go there, so he ran away."

Leah hid the anger that suddenly flared inside her. Would anyone but an unfeeling monster do such a thing to an old man at Christmas?

For the boy's sake, she forced a reasonable tone into her voice. "Well, I'd be willing to bet that by the time you get home your grandfather will be there waiting for you. Now, what we have to do first is get you home. It's too cold to be out here. What is your name?"

"Spencer."

"Spencer what?"

"Spencer Carruthers. I'm eight and a half."

"I'm Leah, Spencer. I'm twenty-seven and a half. It's very nice to meet you."

Once again, he gave her boots a quiet appraisal, then smiled for the first time. "Me, too. What was in the box?"

"Mittens."

"Where are they now?"

"I gave them all away to people who can't afford to buy any."

"How come you did that?"

"I like to help people."

"Oh."

"Where do you live, Spencer?"

"Fifty-two sixteen Alabama Avenue."

"Good. You know, you'd be surprised how many people forget their own address."

Affronted, Spencer sat up straight on the bench. "I've known my address since I was three."

"That's a good thing to know. You must be a very smart boy."

"My dad says I'm too smart for my own good." He frowned and looked at Leah with piercing blue eyes. "What does that mean?"

"Well," she said, "I guess it means that sometimes knowing too much can get you into trouble. I'm sure he just worries about you."

Spencer shook his head. "He doesn't worry about me. He only worries about work and *his* friends."

Memories could haunt as well as please. She knew that only too well. And those of a little girl who never found the right way to make her parents notice her were haunting her now. Always too busy. "Let's find a phone and call your parents," she suggested.

"I don't have parents," he said, jutting out a defiant chin. "Just a dad. And I already told you, he only cares about work."

The twinge of sadness stayed with her. She picked up the box, and the boy followed her. "My dad was like that sometimes," she said.

Spencer regarded her with new interest. "Really?"

"Really."

Obviously deciding that she was okay, he said, "You want to know my phone number?"

"Yes, I do, but why don't you wait until we're closer to a phone? I might forget it."

"How come?"

She laughed, then lowered her voice to a whisper. "They say it comes from getting older."

"You don't look as old as my grandpa."

She cleared her throat. "No, I—I'm sure I'm not quite that old."

They crossed the street and headed toward the phone booth on the corner. "Pop remembers everything. He remembers all the names of our cousins and old friends he used to have when he was my age. He remembers jokes and stories. He remembers everything."

"Then I'm sure he'll remember how to get home."

"Well, he doesn't remember stuff like that so good. Just things way back. Do you live around here?"

"Only a couple of blocks away." She suppressed a new round of shivers and made a mental note to carry a spare coat from now on. "I tell you what, we'll give your father a call and we'll go make some hot chocolate and wait for him to pick you up."

"I know how to make hot chocolate. Pop taught me how. You take milk and put it in a pan. Then you heat it up. Then you pour in chocolate syrup and you stir it up with a spoon. Pop always tries to pour it in a cup, but it misses, so I showed him how you could dip the cup in the pan.''

"Well, you can show me how to do that, too."

"Okay." He held her coat around his body and smiled up at her. "I'm glad I found you."

Leah studied the boy walking briskly at her side. This one, she felt intuitively, was special. "I'm glad you did, too."

"Does this mean we're friends?"

"Absolutely."

"I have lots of friends at school, but I've got room for you, too."

She didn't want to let it feel too good, but it did. An eight-year-old had room for her, space in his heart for Leah Johnson. "Are there children your age in your neighborhood?"

"Some, but they all go to the school down the street. My dad makes me go to dumb old Parkhill."

"Private school?"

"Yes, and I hate it. It's so stupid. They make you wear these dumb uniforms."

"I went to private schools, too."

"You did? Didn't you hate them?"

"Sometimes I didn't like it and sometimes I did."

"Yeah, me too. My dad says I'll get a better education there, but I don't care about that. He's got a good education and all he does is work. I'm going to go to school just long enough so I don't have to work all the time."

Leah laughed. "Good luck, kiddo."

"I mean it. He doesn't have any fun."

Leah thought she had Spencer's father pegged pretty well, and she didn't much care for the image that came to mind. A workaholic. A man who wants to get an old man out of his hair. A father who lets his child run around town unsupervised. Yeah, she had him pegged, all right. But, for the boy's sake, she didn't want to sound too harsh. "Maybe he enjoys his work, Spencer, did you think of that? Maybe it's fun for him."

"Nah, I don't think so. He works all the time because Grandfather Constance expects him to."

"This is your other grandfather?"

"Yeah, my mom's dad. He's my dad's boss. My mom doesn't live with us anymore. My dad's pretty mad about that."

Leah had started to say that she was sorry, assuming the mother had died, but when Spencer said his dad was mad about it, she wondered. She didn't have to wonder long.

"She left us 'cause she doesn't love us anymore. She found somebody else to love."

Leah looked down at the boy walking beside her. His eyes were directed straight ahead, his chin set forward, his mouth tight.

Leah had set out this morning, like every morning, to save the world from itself. Now it was down to one little boy. For her, it was a matter of being equal to the task. And she never doubted for a moment that she would not succeed. But then, she hadn't met Spencer's father, Mark Carruthers.

THE FIRST THING that annoyed Mark about Leah Johnson's house was that it was attached to the DeHaven Center. Memories, sharp and jagged, pierced him like an icy wind. He tucked his head into the collar of his coat to ward off a chill that had never left him, no matter what the weather. All the while he had been growing up, he had never been warm. The north wind had howled angrily through the plank walls of their house and rattled the screens against the doors and windows. Once or twice a year, he and Pop would make a trip to the DeHaven Center for a new pair of long underwear or a winter cap. It was never anything but a humiliating experience for Mark. It crystallized what he was. He was too poor to buy new. He had to depend on society's discards.

After leaving home for college, he told himself he'd never come back to this part of town. And he hadn't. Not until today. Not until that woman called him. Called him and told him she had his son.

The second thing about Leah Johnson that irritated him was that he couldn't find her doorbell through the confused tangle of pine garland that was draped everywhere. He should have brought a machete. Growing impatient with the search, he rapped his fist loudly against the thick wooden door.

It was opened by a slim, wide-eyed woman holding a plate of fresh-baked cookies. The sounds of someone banging noisily on a piano traveled around the door.

Smells of warm ginger and cinnamon reached his nose and threw his mind temporarily off balance. He had spent hours worrying about Spencer and Pop, until finally anger had taken over. She had called with the news. His housekeeper gave him the message and, furious, he left right away. To have to come to this part of town and to subject himself to painful memories of his childhood had added more fuel to the fire. Inexplicably, the anger was set aside for the moment, and he now focused on the sights and sounds and scents before him.

The woman was younger than he had expected. Late twenties, probably. Her brown hair tumbled carelessly around her face in thick strands of curls. She wore little or no makeup, and a crescent of freckles arched across the bridge of her nose, fading away when they reached her cheeks. But it was her eyes that held him captivated.

Though hers were a radiant golden brown and Spencer's were a vivid sky blue, there was something about them that immediately reminded Mark of his son. They held a hint of laughter and zest, he quickly decided, something he felt that was sorely lacking in himself. Or perhaps something that was directed at him. Was she laughing at him? he wondered.

Spencer often had that mischievous glint in his eyes, as if devilish thoughts were starting to sprout and bear fruit in his head. It usually spelled big trouble for Mark.

Leah was surprised by the man at her door. She had expected some sort of two-headed monster who ate old men and little children for breakfast. This man looked slightly befuddled.

"Hello," she said. "Are you Mr. Carruthers?"

Mark steeled himself against the warm, inviting lilt of her voice. She had caused him enough trouble already, she and Spencer and Pop.

"Are my son and father here?" he asked coolly.

"Your son is. Pop seems to have disappeared. Come on in."

It struck him as odd that she had used Pop's name, as if she had settled herself into their lives like some long-lost cousin. He glanced at her. She was wearing an oversize sweatshirt, jeans and combat boots. She *wasn't* a cousin, was she? The question drifted away when he stepped into the room and was immediately assaulted by a baffling array of stimuli. Across the room, Spencer was happily pounding on an old upright piano while he crammed one cookie after another into his mouth. He glanced up at Mark, but his mouth was too packed with food to form even a greeting.

The room was a carnival of distractions. Books and newspapers and unfinished craft projects were strewn about haphazardly. The furniture—functional, well-worn pieces—reminded Mark of the kind his mountain relatives had in their houses. The kind dumped out on the sides of country roads. And the Christmas decorations! Why, the place was so packed full of tinsel and holly and trimmings there was hardly enough room to breathe, much less walk. The woman set the plate of cookies on the counter beside a half-eaten pan of fudge. The counter separated the living room from the tiny kitchen, and he spied a dish drain full of dishes. He knew the type. Nothing ever put away. Life in disarray and blamed on lack of time.

It all came to a head in that moment, all the worry and searching and frantic thoughts that had catapulted through his head for the past few hours. It all came to a head as he stood, unsettled, in Leah Johnson's chaotic living room that smelled of apples and cinnamon and sweet Christmas cookies.

"Do you have any idea the trouble you've caused me?" he growled at his son.

Spencer's small fingers ceased their hammering against the keys. He swiveled on the bench and swallowed the last bite of cookie. "Me?"

"Yes, you." Mark flicked an angry glance at Leah that included her in the summation. "How could you and Pop take off like that without leaving any word?"

"Pop left. I just followed him."

"I am having a dinner party tonight. The guests are probably already arriving at the house. You have completely disrupted..." Mark frowned at his son. "What do you mean, Pop left?"

Spencer hugged his arms across his chest, and his mouth was tight and rigid.

Mark took a menacing step forward. "Don't you clam up on me now. Where's Pop?"

While he had been snarling at his son, Leah had done her own quick but thorough summation of Mark Carruthers. Beneath his mask of indignation, he was a very handsome man. She had expected an older, taller version of Spencer, but Mark was very different from his son. His hair was dark brown, and the blue of his eyes was more intense than that of his son's. Like the sky before a storm, they were. His lean features were made sharp by the anger that tightened them. His mouth was stretched and flattened into a grim line.

When Leah felt the silence between father and son had gone on long enough, she interjected. "He didn't want to live in a retirement home."

Mark spun around, focusing his wrath on her. "I beg your pardon?"

She remained unflinching and resolute before his ire. "I said, he apparently didn't want to live in a retirement home, so he ran away."

Mark's eyes slipped from Spencer to Leah and back to Spencer. His son received the next verbal blow. "I don't believe this! I'm late for my own dinner party, and you're out running around the city, blabbing our personal family problems to—to..." He waved his hand toward Leah. "To strangers."

Spencer's sense of guilt, while short-lived, was very real. "Sorry, sir," he mumbled and ducked his head.

Mark, realizing he could not, in good conscience, continue to yell at a guilt-stricken child, turned to Leah. She was sitting on a bar stool, munching on a piece of fudge as if all was right with the world.

"And you," he growled, ransacking his mind for something about her to criticize. "My son does not need to be eating all that sweet junk."

It was several seconds before she finished chewing and swallowed. "He looked hungry." She picked up the pan of fudge and held it out. "You look hungry, too. Want one?" She frowned. "Something wrong?"

Wrong? Mark was as taut as a rubber band that was about to snap. *Wrong?* His father was missing. His son had been wandering the streets alone. He wasn't at home to host his own dinner party. And this impudent woman, with laughing eyes and combat boots, this stranger who seemed to know their whole life story, was calmly offering him candy.

He had trouble getting the words out. "Miss Johnson, I appreciate your help with my son. Thank you for calling me. We are going to leave now. I have to find my father. Goodbye."

Leah stood and stepped close to him, throwing him even more off balance. Her eyebrows pulled together as she scrutinized his face. "You don't look so good, Mr. Carruthers. I think you'd better sit down and let me get you some herbal tea." She grabbed his arm and led him to the couch. "Here."

There was nothing timid about her hand on his arm. Her grip was firm and assertive. But he wasn't about to let her push him around. "I don't think—" he sputtered, but the next thing he knew, he was surrounded by a pile of fat pillows and overstuffed cushions on the couch. Two unruly cats jumped into his lap. One began sucking on the sleeve of Mark's jacket, the other purred like a motorboat in his ear.

"She was weaned too soon," informed Spencer, plopping down beside his dad to pet the cat who was drooling on Mark's coat.

"Listen, I really have to go," said Mark, pushing both cats to the floor. He tried to shove off from the sea of cushions, but he couldn't get enough leverage.

"Nonsense, Mr. Carruthers," said Leah, as she stuck a warm cup in his hands.

He fell back into the sofa and stared at his captor. "How did you do that so fast?"

"I had it in the microwave already."

"Oh." Why was he letting her hold him prisoner like this? Letting her force him to drink her tea? He had guests at the house waiting for him. He reluctantly took a sip of the tea and made a face. "Yuck! What is this?"

She smiled pleasantly, as if he had just praised her tea rather than criticized it. "It's my own concoction."

"I never would have guessed," he murmured dryly. He didn't know quite what to make of this woman, but he was almost positive he didn't particularly like her. First of all, she lived on the wrong side of town. Second of all, she was too cheerful about it. To top it off, she had the type of looks—the unsophisticated prettiness that he had stopped appreciating a long time ago. So why couldn't he stop staring at her now?

"Isn't this house neat!" cried Spencer, jumping up from the couch and darting from one thing to another in the room. "See, she has a *real* Christmas tree! Isn't it neat? And look at all these cool decorations!"

Mark took stock of the hodgepodge of furnishings and decorations. There was not a cubic inch of empty space in the room. "Yeah, neat," he said as he forced himself to take another sip of witch's brew. "Spence, where did Pop go?"

"To live under a bridge."

Mark choked on the tea. "A bridge! What are you talking about?"

Spencer spun away from the tree and railed at his father. "It's all your fault!" he cried. "He doesn't want to go live at any old folks' home. He wants to live with us. Why can't he stay with us? Why are you always so mean!"

"Spencer," said Leah, taking him gently by the shoulders. "That is no way to talk to your father. Now, I think you should apologize to him."

Mark stared dumbfounded at the two of them. He was shocked by Spencer's outburst, but he was even more shocked by the audacity of the woman. A virtual stranger, giving orders to *his* son. There was something so damn infuriating about her, he found it difficult to even respond. "I really don't think you have—"

"I'm sorry, Daddy," said Spencer humbly, then he leaned over and gave Mark a big hug. Tea sloshed from the cup onto Mark's hand, but he didn't feel a thing.

He was overwhelmed. He was numb. It was too much. The situation, the woman, the house, the smells of Christmas. He had enough chaos in his life without someone like her coming along to clutter and befuddle it up any more.

Mark placed the cup on the coffee table and, with great effort, managed to get up. "I really do have to go. I have guests at home. Spencer, get your coat."

"I don't have one. Leah let me wear hers."

His eyes took in the scene. She and Spencer were grinning at each other with a familiarity that made Mark feel as if he was the one who was out in the cold, alone, without a coat. He knew it was irrational, but it made him dislike Leah Johnson even more. Spencer never smiled at him that way. It made him even angrier to realize how irrational he was being about this whole thing. It was the messy house, he figured, that set his teeth on edge. He liked things neat and orderly.

Or maybe all these suffocating smells of Christmas that kept tugging long-forgotten memories—maybe that was what bugged him.

"If you need help finding your father," she said, when he turned toward the front door. "Just call me."

But then—

Maybe it was her.

"No," he said. "You really don't have to involve—"

"Leah knows lots of people who live on the streets," chimed in Spencer. "She gives 'em mittens."

Mark wasn't even going to try to figure that one out. People who lived on the east side of town were all strange. "I'm sure Pop will find his way home," he said. "He's a grown man. Probably just wants a bit of freedom."

"I don't think so, Mr. Carruthers," said Leah with a certainty that almost drove him up the wall. He felt as if she had scraped her fingernails down a chalkboard.

"You don't think so?" he asked with deceptive calm.

"No."

"How would you know, Miss Johnson? You don't even know my father."

"Oh, I told her everything about him," said Spencer. "Everything about you, too."

Mark's upper row of teeth ground into his lower. "Is that right?"

"It sounds like your father is hurt," suggested Leah helpfully. "From what he told Spencer, it looks like he might actually plan to live on the streets."

"That's patently absurd!" barked Mark. "I have a big house. He has his own room. This is utter nonsense. He's too—well, he's too old for it."

"Well, if he doesn't come home," she said, "let me know. I might be able to help you locate him."

He couldn't keep the surly tone from his voice. "Oh? And how is that?" He had lost control of the situation, the moment, his father and his son. He felt as if her tea had congealed and was stuck in his throat.

"I have contacts at the missions," she answered. "And at some of the social-service agencies. I do volunteer work with the homeless and at the De-Haven Center next door. I might be able to help.''

The chill slid through his body. A volunteer at the DeHaven Center. Some bleeding-heart do-gooder who took pity on the poor and the bedraggled. He felt transparent, exposed, as if she could see straight through him to his past. He wondered if that was why she had taken pity on his son.

''You've helped enough,'' he said through clenched teeth. ''Now, let's go, Spencer.''

''I don't want to go,'' the boy whined, pulling back. ''I like it here. Isn't this neat? A *real* tree, Dad. And look at all the decorations. She taught me how to play 'Jingle Bells' on the piano. Want to hear it?''

Mark's voice dropped into the danger zone, each syllable exaggerated. ''Not now, Spencer. We are going. Say goodbye to the lady.''

''Bye, Leah.''

Mark noticed that she positively beamed at the boy like an old friend. ''Bye, kiddo. You can come see me any time.''

''My son doesn't go out on his own,'' said Mark. ''At least, not normally. And we live a long way from this part of town.''

''You can bring me here, Dad.''

''Yes, you're welcome any time,'' she said again to Spencer.

''Can I play the piano again when I come?''

''Sure.''

Mark's patience had reached the breaking point. And he felt as if he was suffocating. He had to get out of here. Now. "Out, Spencer."

"Oh, by the way, Mr. Carruthers," Leah said as he passed by. "Merry Christmas."

Mark stared briefly at the pretty woman who had rescued his son and who had warmed him with her tea. But he didn't answer. He just wanted to get away from her and this place as quickly as possible. He didn't dare look back.

But all the way to the car, he had to listen to Spencer rattling on about the neat lady and her neat house and her neat tree. "A real tree, Dad."

Real. Is that what she was? Mark wondered. If so, that was probably why he didn't like her. He had no place in his life for real women. That type of reality was something he wanted no part of. He had created his own.

Leah stood in the lighted doorway and watched them leave. She felt a curious light-headedness, as if she were standing a few inches above the threshold. He was a handsome man, she admitted, but looks were not enough to send her into a tailspin. And she had been around troubled men before. No, maybe it was because his son was trying so hard to gain his father's attention. Maybe because she had been there. She knew exactly what that boy was going through.

She hadn't succeeded with her own father, but maybe, just maybe, she could help Spencer Carruthers succeed with his. Equal to the task. That's all that was involved. Besides, the man needed something done about him. If anybody ever needed fixing, it was him. She'd wished him a Merry Christmas and he hadn't even answered. She could see she had her work cut out for her, but that was okay. She thrived on challenges.

Besides, no grinch was safe around Leah Johnson.

The question was—was she safe around a grinch who looked as good as Mark Carruthers?

Chapter Four

"Bad form, Mark," Abel said in a chastising voice. "The guests were here thirty minutes before you. What on earth happened?"

Mark had rushed in with Spencer a few minutes ago, thrown his coat in the study and hurried into the living room where his guests were admiring the sculpture. Abel had, thank goodness, taken over in his absence and had fixed drinks for everyone. Everyone included General Boynton, aide to the Joint Chiefs of Staff, his wife, and Air Force colonels Lawford and Sills and their wives. Then there was Richard Hatterfield, lobbyist, congressional aide, consultant and full-time hustler. He declined to bring his wife.

The military men were on their second drinks, while Hatterfield was on his third. Abel was having his first private word with Mark.

"Minor emergency," said Mark. "Pop has decided to run away from home."

"What? Today?"

"Yes."

"Did you talk to him about the retirement home?"

Mark nodded. "That's why he took off." He shook his head. "It really hurt him, Abel."

The older man rested a proprietary hand on Mark's shoulder. "It had to be done. It's the best thing for him . . . and for you."

Mark saw the look of complete confidence in Abel's face, the expression of absolute right. He wished he felt the same. "You're right."

"Of course I am," said Abel. "Now, should we have everyone sit down?"

Though the party was in his home, Mark took his cues from his father-in-law. If Abel said it was time to sit down and serve dinner, then that was exactly what time it was.

Mark had first met Abel a month after he started working for Constance Aeronautics. He had been working on a design for a contract the company had with the military when he got the call to go to the president's office. Impressed with the design, Abel wanted to meet the new recruit who had drawn it, and from that moment forward, Mark Carruthers had become Abel Constance's "boy."

He was moved up the corporate ladder at lightning speed. And along with the new role came perks and obligations that a twenty-five-year-old from Blue Mountain had never imagined. He was ushered and coerced from one social event to another. He learned golf and tennis so he could play with Abel and his cronies. He took a public speaking course so he would not embarrass himself in front of Abel's more learned friends. He went into hock to buy a new car and to move into a nicer apartment on the west side of town, an apartment with Abel's stamp of approval.

He was invited to private parties, wined and dined at the finest restaurants. And, as perk of all perks, Mark Carruthers, whiz kid of the aeronautics world and fast tracker of the company, was introduced to Abel Constance's beautiful socialite daughter, Angela. Many of Mark's co-workers had been envious of his meteoric rise in the company and of his direct route to the president of the firm, but when he married the boss's daughter and a month later was promoted to senior vice-president of Constance Aeronautics, resentment replaced the envy.

Mark was a good engineer and a valuable asset to the company. Not one employee could argue with that. But absolutely no one made senior vice-president in three years. No one, that is, who didn't marry into it.

Mark ushered his dinner guests into the dining room then disappeared briefly into the kitchen. "We're ready now, Clara."

When Angela had been with him, she had handled all the party preparations with great aplomb. She had grown up among the glitter and pomp. She had known exactly what to do in every situation. Now that she was gone, Mark had to depend on hired help to do the job. But Abel had found Clara for him, and she had worked out extremely well . . .

Except, of course, that Pop had said he was teaching her how to make beds properly. Mark didn't know why that struck him as funny, but it did.

Clara glared sharply at him when he laughed.

He cleared away the smile. "Everything under control?"

"Of course."

Yes, he thought, everything was under control. Everything, that is, except his own personal life. His eighty-two-year-old father was out wandering the streets alone on the coldest night of the year. Spencer was upstairs pouting in his room because Mark had run Pop off. His wife and the mother of his child had fled to New Mexico for what she referred to as "a life with *real* passion." And Mark was left with dinner guests he didn't really care about and a father-in-law who lacked control over his daughter but had increased his control over his son-in-law and star employee.

"You really must take advantage of the retreat we have in Colorado Springs. I can see to it that you have access."

The invitation was issued by Hatterfield, but the colonels looked uncomfortable. After all, it was for officers only.

Subtle undercurrents ran throughout dinner meetings like this, but Mark had lost all interest in this one. He kept picturing an icy bridge beneath a shrouded sky. An old man, smoking his last cigar, his coat inadequate, his fly undone.

"Golf, swimming, tennis, great food at the club."

And that woman. In his mind, he kept reaching for a warm cup, offered by her, served with a relaxed smile.

The chicken Kiev Clara served was excellent as always, its goodness confirmed by the mask of pleasure plastered over Abel's face. It was another roaring success. Another Brownie point for Mark. Another rung in the ladder that climbed endlessly and forever upward.

"It's all in a strong defense," said Boynton. "And this new Five-O fighter will solidify our position."

"Wait till the committee gets a load of the price, though," inserted Hatterfield. "You're sure going to need me then."

"What about that, Constance? What can be done about the costs on this thing?"

"You've seen the design. This one has it all." He looked to Mark for some input, but Mark couldn't get his mind on track. "What about it?"

Mark knew how important this contract was to Abel and to the company, so he made an attempt to sound enthusiastic. "Maybe the thing can be reworked a bit. I'll see what I can do."

"If anyone can do it," bragged Abel, "it's this boy."

Mark grew uncomfortable, knowing what was in store. It was Abel's favorite story, the whole Horatio Alger bit. It didn't seem to matter that every time Abel started in, Mark was embarrassed. He didn't want the world to see where he had come from. He didn't want to be the curiosity show, the two-headed reptile boy who had defied the odds and had risen from the muck of poverty. He wanted the world to see the man he had created, to see him as they might one of their own sons. But Abel loved an audience, and this story never failed to keep them spellbound.

During dessert Colonel Sills's wife began the stalk. She no longer saw her host as a refined and slightly mundane young engineer who was throwing a dinner party. No. She saw what Abel had created in her mind. Something wild, untamed, forbidden. But didn't she know, he wasn't like that anymore. The boy of Abel's fable was not any more real than the one who sat before her now.

Mark tried to pretend he didn't notice the woman's advances. He remembered so well the first night he met Angela. It was a party, thrown by her doting father, for her twenty-first birthday. No other man even close to her age had been invited. Mark was it. The one and only. The sacrificial lamb. Abel had made sure of it.

At some point during the evening, Abel had pulled him aside and said, "She needs someone like you, Mark. Someone who's lived both sides of the track. And, believe me, you need her. If anyone can tame you, Carruthers, she can."

And she had. The wild, unruly wolf from the mountains had been tamed. Angela did not care for what she referred to as his "animal instincts and drive." She wanted him as quiet, refined and methodical in his lovemaking as he was in lining up a putt on the eighteenth green. She didn't like the wild lawless streak in him. He learned quickly to suppress it for her sake.

It was not a marriage made in heaven, but rather a marriage made in the boardroom. The fact that he was on the fast track in the aeronautics firm, and the fact that Daddy approved of him wholeheartedly, insured her legacy to the family-owned company. It also gave Mark a solid foothold in Abel Constance's world.

Mark set down his fork and let himself be captured by the tantalizing curve of Mrs. Sills's mouth. It had been a long time since he'd been with anyone like her. A long time since he'd been with anyone at all. Others answered invitations like this one. Why shouldn't he? She was beautiful, sophisticated, obviously available.

A warm cup of coffee replaced his dessert plate. His fingers touched the saucer, and the woman's image was swept away by another wholly unexpected one.

Eyes with a different kind of invitation. Brown eyes that laughed and crinkled at the edges. Brown eyes that sent heat to places he had forgotten existed. Eyes that threatened to change everything.

When the doorbell rang, the cup rattled against his saucer. His heart accelerated, and the woman across the table vanished into thin air.

Pop, he thought with an anticipation that surprised him. He had come home.

He jumped up from his chair before Abel's censuring glance was able to capture him.

"I'm sure your housekeeper will take care of it, Mark."

Mark sat and reached for his coffee. He didn't dare look at Mrs. Sills. Maybe it was true that you could take the boy out of the country, but you couldn't take the country out of the boy. That's what they said. And no matter how long he had been away or how hard he had worked to lose the habits, they still crept up on him. He still found himself saying "Yes, ma'am" even to the maid. He still had trouble sitting on a made-up bed. He still cringed when someone said, "Help yourself to a beer," because it meant he'd have to open their icebox—a strict taboo on the mountain. That kind of etiquette sent one scurrying to the door when someone came calling.

The rules of country etiquette had been ingrained too well in him. His mother had done her job, and Angela had failed at undoing it.

Over the sonorous clink of fine crystal and the light ping of silver spoons against china coffee cups, Mark heard Clara open the front door. Though no one else seemed to feel it, Mark was hit by a blast of wintry air that shot through the house. He cringed inwardly at the sound of boots tamping ice loose on the front step.

He knew. Somehow he knew who had arrived. And it certainly wasn't Pop.

"Mr. Carruthers is entertaining guests at the moment," he heard Clara say.

"That's okay," the lilting voice answered. "Spencer's the one I want to see."

"Spencer?"

"Yes. It's about his grandfather."

Abel glanced at Mark with a questioning look.

Mark stood up. "Excuse me," he said to his guests. "I'll be right back." He avoided Abel's eyes as he left the room, but he knew they were on him. And he knew they were no longer pleased.

When he stepped into the entryway, Leah Johnson was slipping off a navy wool pea coat. Clara was reluctantly waiting to take it from her, but Leah tossed it onto the brass coatrack in the corner.

"Hi," she said when she saw Mark. Clara eyed him with a look of censure that was identical to Abel's.

"It's okay, Clara. I'll take care of it. You might want to go pour more coffee." There was that slight hint of question in his voice, as if she would mind. That inability to rise above subservience, even with the domestic help. It was the sense somewhere deep inside him that said if he spoke sharply to a woman, if he gave one direct demand or order, his father would reach out and cuff his ears.

Clara didn't cuff his ears. She simply said, "Yes, sir," and went to the kitchen.

"Hi," said Leah again when they were alone. "I don't want to disturb your dinner." She peered around the corner to see if she could get a look at the guests. "I just came to see Spencer."

Mark's eyes took in her appearance. She still had on the combat boots and jeans, but she had replaced the sweatshirt with a huge forest-green sweater that hung almost to her knees. It accentuated the deep brown of her eyes. She still wore no makeup, and her hair was tousled by the wind. But she smelled great, like fresh linens hung on the line in spring.

And there was not a whiff of artifice about her.

The minute Mark felt his pulse begin to rise, he forcefully shut all systems down. "What do you want to see Spencer for?"

She had convinced herself that she had come to see Spencer only. Now, looking at Mark, she wondered if she had been completely truthful with herself. Just looking at him, she felt a hot July wind blow over her. He was dressed in an impeccable dark suit, but a bare-chested man on a windy cliff lay just beneath the surface. She didn't at all understand her reaction to him. It was a frightening thing, like a fresh cut that lies open and raw to the elements but does not yet sense pain.

She pulled in the reins on her system. "I thought I'd see if he could give me a photograph of Pop. It might help in finding him."

The guests' laughter filtered into the entry hall. "Of course, what with the sound of that, he must be home."

Mark had the grace to look embarrassed. "He's not home."

"Oh, I see."

"I doubt it."

Leah cleared her throat. "Well, I don't want to keep you from your party, so maybe I could just talk to Spencer. Is he upstairs?"

She had been in his house for less than five minutes and already she was irritating him. He supposed she thought she was welcome to traipse all over his house as if she lived there. He was just about to tell her what he thought when an excited voice hollered down from the top of the stairs.

Spencer bounded down the stairs like a puppy dog. "Hi, Leah!"

Mark scowled. "Keep your voice down, Spencer. We have guests."

Abel charged like General Patton into the hallway. "Mark, what's going on? Is everything all right?"

"Yes, yes. Everything's—fine. Spencer was just coming—this is just the woman who found—" *God, I'm babbling like an idiot.* "Miss Johnson, I'd like for you to meet Abel Constance, Spencer's grandfather. Abel, this is Leah Johnson. She is, uh . . ." How on earth was he supposed to describe her? As the woman who found his son wandering loose in the city? As a bleeding heart from the east side of town? As a tacky housekeeper? As the cookie lady? What? "She's a friend," he finally said. It wasn't true, he knew. She could certainly not qualify as a friend. He didn't even know her. But the truth would be too unsettling to try to explain. Even to himself. "Of Spencer's," he added.

Leah stepped forward and confidently held out her hand to the large man with scowl lines permanently etched at the sides of his mouth. She was glad she wasn't the timid type. If she were, Abel Constance would have scared her to death.

"I'm Spencer's music teacher, Mr. Constance. And it's a pleasure to meet you."

Music teacher? Mark smirked, unsure whether to thank her for saving the moment or call her a bold-faced liar and boot her out into the cold.

"Music teacher." Abel smiled, relief adding bulk to the sag of his cheeks. "How nice. Mark, you didn't tell me you were having Spencer take music lessons."

"Well, I—"

"On what instrument?"

"Piano," said Leah.

Abel frowned. "You don't have a piano, Mark, do you?"

"No. Not yet. But, I—I suppose we'll have to be getting one."

"We are?" cried Spencer. "Oh, boy! A piano."

"Well, of course," said Abel. "You should have told me you wanted a piano, Spencer. I would have gotten one for you. I'll make sure one is ordered to-morrow."

Mark couldn't believe this! The whole situation had gotten completely out of hand. "You really don't have to do that, Abel."

"My grandson wants a piano, Mark. You really should have told me." The affront was evident in the straight back. "I will go back to the table now. I hope you, too, will come along. We certainly don't want a breach of etiquette on your part to quash this deal with the Pentagon."

"Yes, of course. I'll be right there." When Abel was gone from sight, Mark's eyes closed briefly. He felt as if he'd been run over by a tank. When he opened his eyes, Leah Johnson was still there, every sweet-smelling and annoying inch of her. "Music teacher?"

"You looked like you were having trouble explaining to Mr. Constance who I was. I thought I would help you out. And—" she smiled sweetly "—I take it he is not Pop."

"No way," said Spencer before Mark could answer. "He's nothing like Pop."

Mark scowled at the boy. "You watch how you talk about your grandfather, son. Especially after you just conned him into buying you a piano." Mark looked at Leah. "No, he is not Pop. But I was not having trouble explaining who you were."

"My mistake, then," she said with that same smile.

Why did she do that? Why was she always smiling, even while being caustic? He sighed, deflated by the tedium of the dinner party and by the fact that Pop was missing and by the constant need to please Abel and now by Leah Johnson standing in his entryway, looking great in Salvation Army castoffs. He knew it was a crazy thought, but he almost wished for one brief moment that she was here to see him.

"I have to get back to my guests. I don't really think you need a photograph of Pop, Miss Johnson. I'm sure he'll turn up tonight. This has all been blown way out of proportion."

"You're probably right," she said. "I just thought in case he didn't, I'd have the picture."

"But he will."

"I'm sure he will."

He glared.

She smiled.

He breathed through his nose. "Spence, find Miss Johnson a photograph." Without another word, he spun around and returned to his dinner party. But he could no longer relax. His jaw was tight, his stomach churning. He tried to make pleasant conversation while Spencer and Miss Johnson were off causing who knew what kind of havoc in the rest of the house.

Chapter Five

The dinner party wound to a quick close, whether because of his desertion from the table or his stilted conversation Mark didn't know. Nor, at this point, did he care.

Still, like the perfect host he was expected to be, he smiled and shook hands with each of his departing guests, promising the colonels Lawford and Sills that he would be meeting with them again in a couple of days.

After they were gone, Abel summed it all up. "It was an—interesting evening. Not without its moments."

Understatement of the year, thought Mark.

"Do work on this, Mark. Try to see what cuts can be made to hold the manufacturing costs down."

"I will."

"And try to get these pesky domestic difficulties wrapped up."

Domestic difficulties. Abel left, and Mark went to the bar to fix a drink. Pop was out in the cold, and his father-in-law thought of it as a pesky domestic problem.

The outside sounds of winter were shut off from the inside. Behind him, in the dining room, he could hear Clara picking up cups and saucers and carrying them into the kitchen. And from Spencer's room, he heard voices from the radio. He kept his eyes closed and breathed deeply. It was several long seconds before he began to frown. Voices. They weren't coming from a radio. That was Spencer talking and laughing. And it was Leah Johnson's voice.

Mark took the stairs two at a time. He found them walking down the hallway from Pop's bedroom. They were holding hands.

"Hi, Dad," said Spencer. "I've been showing Leah the house. I showed her Pop's room. We got a picture of him. And I showed her my room. We looked at all my stuff. Then I showed her the bathroom. And now I'm going to show her your room."

He didn't want Leah Johnson seeing his room. In fact, he didn't want her seeing any of his house. But he wasn't sure how he could tactfully steer her out into the night. Besides, Spencer was already leading her toward his room.

"That's okay, Spencer," she was saying. "I think you've showed me enough for tonight."

Behind her, Mark heaved a sigh of relief. How had she known? Was it that evident on his face? Somehow she had sensed what he was feeling.

Stopping in the hallway, waiting for him, she held up the photograph. "Pop looks like a great guy."

Mark let the tension flow from his body. "Yeah."

"Spencer showed me the photo album. You look like your mother."

"I suppose so."

"She was a beautiful woman."

Spencer had obviously also told Leah Johnson that his mother was dead. So she knew almost everything about them. Who had left whom. Who was dead. Who was good. Who was bad. She knew it all.

"Well," she said, clutching the photograph.

"Well," he said.

"I guess I'd better be going."

"Yes."

"Not yet," whined Spencer. "Can't we make some hot chocolate?"

"Don't you think it's past your bedtime?" asked Mark.

"No. It's early. And I'm hungry. Pop and I always fix a snack at night."

Silence settled over the house while Mark bore the weight of Spencer's resentment. Only the faint sounds from Clara in the kitchen drifted up the stairs.

"I guess a cup of hot chocolate would taste pretty good," said Mark, hoping to lighten the air around him. No one had to tell him that he had blown it with Pop. But the idea of Windward Estates had just been a suggestion. He hadn't meant for Pop to run away like that. Really he hadn't.

"Oh, boy!" said Spencer, bumping down the stairs on his bottom. He rushed toward the kitchen. "I'll heat the milk."

The two of them took the stairs at a more sedate pace.

"How was your party?"

"Oh, fine. Fine." Awful. Boring.

They made it to the first floor and headed for the kitchen. "Who were all the Boy Scouts?"

He glanced at her, chuckling. "Those Boy Scouts were top Pentagon officials."

She halted and planted her hands on her waist. A few steps ahead, Mark stopped and looked back quizzically.

"What do you do for a living?" she asked.

"I'm an engineer for Constance Aeronautics. Why?"

Her scowl deepened, and her fists were pressed tightly into her sides. "What are you designing, gun ships?"

Great, he thought. Now he was going to be criticized by her for that, too. "As a matter of fact," he said carefully, "we do have some military contracts."

"Do you sleep well at night?"

"I sleep fine. Look, Miss Johnson, I know you think I'm some sort of ogre for running my father off... and now you obviously think I'm also a warmonger or something, but you really know nothing about me or my father or my son."

"You're absolutely right." She nodded briskly and headed for the kitchen.

He stayed behind for a minute, wondering what she meant by that. Did she mean he was right about her not knowing them? Or did she mean he was right about her thinking him an ogre and a warmonger? God, but she wore him out. He'd known her for—he checked his watch—exactly five hours, and the woman was already making him crazy. What on earth had he done to deserve a visit from her tonight?

When he went into the kitchen, Leah was already helping Spencer pour the milk, and Clara was drying dishes.

"I HOPE YOU DON'T MIND if we dirty a few more dishes, Clara," Mark said, mentally kicking himself as the words came out. What was he apologizing for? It was his house!

"It's your house, Mr. Carruthers," Clara said without looking at him.

Leah smiled at the maid. "Don't worry, Clara, I'll clean up whatever we mess up."

Mark watched the friendly exchange between the two women. That really irked him. And what a joke!

He'd seen Leah Johnson's house. He'd hate to see his kitchen after she finished with it.

Mark sat and stared glumly at the other three bustling around the kitchen as if they were all having a great time. Leah and Spencer put the pan on the stove to heat the milk, and Clara stacked the last of the dishes in the cupboard. She took off her apron and hung it on the hook inside the pantry.

"Are you sure you don't want me to stay and clean this up?" she asked, but when Mark looked over to answer her, he saw that she was asking Leah, not him. He let Leah answer.

"No, we'll manage perfectly. But thank you, Clara."

Thank you, Clara, he grumbled silently. "Good night, Clara," he said, asserting himself as master of the house. "Thank you for your help tonight. The dinner was perfect."

"Good." She looked at Spencer. "I'll see you tomorrow, Spencer."

"Yes'm," he said, but as soon as she was gone, he complained, "Why does she have to look after me?"

"Because there is no one else, that's why."

Spencer slammed a wooden spoon on the counter. "If Pop were here, he could."

With his elbows resting on the table, Mark pinched the bridge of his nose. "I'll look for Pop tomorrow, Spence. I'll find him, okay?"

"That's right, Spencer," said Leah. "Don't you worry about a thing. Because, by tomorrow night, we'll have Pop home where he belongs." She set a cup of steaming cocoa in front of Mark and said, "Right?"

He didn't answer. He just wrapped his fingers around the warm cup and glared at it. What did she know about where Pop belonged? She didn't have to listen to the incessant ramblings of an eighty-two-year-old man. She didn't have to put up with rampant unwanted advice. She didn't have to deal with incurable forgetfulness that caused everything from minor disruptions to dangerous catastrophes. It was as Abel said when he gave Mark the brochure for the retirement home—a man should accept the aging process with grace and dignity. Why couldn't Pop?

Mark took a large gulp from the cup, and it burned a path down his throat.

"So," said Leah, sitting at the table as if she were right at home. "Let's talk about Pop, so we know where to start looking."

Spencer sat opposite Leah and slurped his cocoa through a mound of marshmallows.

Mark's eyes were trained on Leah. The very things about her that were so appealing were also the things that were the most annoying. But how could that be?

She had sidled too easily into their lives. Slipped under his skin. Never had a woman done that in five hours, not in this way. If it were only on the physical plane, he could understand it. But it was something else. Something more.

Maybe it was fatigue that made him so susceptible tonight. All he needed was a good night's sleep. In the morning, she'd be out of his mind completely.

He turned his attention to Spencer. "Did Pop say he was going to stay with one of the cousins?"

Spencer slurped loudly. "Nope. I asked him if he was going to live with Cus'n Cooter, and he said no."

"What about one of the others?"

Spencer glanced at Leah. "We got lots of cus'ns back in the mountains."

"What fun!" she said, sipping her chocolate. "I think it would be great to have lots of relatives."

Mark wished for a hole in the floor to swallow him up. "They're distant cousins. Very distant."

"Daddy doesn't like them," said Spencer.

Mark cringed from the sharp blow. "That's not true! Spencer, you've got to stop saying things like that. Miss Johnson is going to get the wrong idea."

"Oh, I think I have the right idea, Mr. Carruthers."

He turned toward her. "Oh? And what is that?" He was searching for the inevitable disgust or pity in her eyes. It was always one or the other when it was learned where he came from. Funny, but he seemed to find neither in hers.

She looked at Spencer instead of at him. "Your father has a very important job, Spencer. Many people depend on him." Her expression revealed to Mark exactly what she thought of some of those people, but she kept her comments neutral. "He has built a life way over here on this side of town, and he has to live a certain way for his job." She looked at Mark. "Am I right?"

She was right. But why did it sound like some sort of indictment when it came from her lips? He cleared his throat and mumbled a noncommittal answer.

Spencer dunked his marshmallows with his finger. "I just wish we could go see 'em sometimes. It's lots more fun than staying here all the time."

"I know," she agreed. "And especially at Christmas time. This is when families should be together. All the grandparents and cousins and aunts and uncles. Don't you agree?" she asked Mark.

She was laying a trap for him. He could see it clear as day, but he wasn't sure how to steer around it. "I suppose."

"Really!" cried Spencer. "You mean we can go visit them?"

"I didn't say that, Spence. I've got a lot of things going right now. Maybe sometime in the new year. We'll see."

"Oh," Spencer said, dejected. "Sure. You always say that. We never do, though."

"The first thing we have to do is find Pop. What else did he say to you before he left?"

"He said he wasn't going to go live with a bunch of old people in some stupid home. To that stupid place you were going to make him go."

"I wasn't going to make him go anywhere, Spence." Mark looked defensively at Leah. "I wasn't."

"I believe you."

"I don't," said Spencer.

Mark slammed his hand on the table. "Well, you can just go on up to bed then, young man. I won't have that kind of talk."

Spencer slammed back his chair and ran from the room. Ghostly anger and hurt remained behind.

Mark let out a long, tired breath. "Damn. I didn't handle that right. As usual."

Leah studied the dark circles beneath Mark's eyes, and she wished she could touch them and make them go away. "It must be hard to raise a child all by yourself."

He rested his forearms on the table and stared at the marshmallows floating in Spencer's cup. "Yeah," he said quietly. "It is."

So she did know it all. He had suspected as much. But oddly enough, it seemed natural that she would ask and he would answer. While Leah Johnson could be as irritating as a flea in a dog's ear, there was something about her that made it easy to say what was on his mind.

"I don't do a very good job of it, I'm afraid."

"I disagree," she said. "Spencer's a great kid. And he loves you very much."

He looked at her. She had only met Spencer this afternoon. How could she possibly know something like that? "How do you know?"

"It's so obvious, Mark. All he talks about is you. At my house, today, it was 'my dad this and my dad that'. He worships the ground you walk on."

The way Leah Johnson said his name, it was as if she had known him forever. He couldn't remember when his name on a woman's lips had sounded so nice. So easy. The golden brown of her eyes beneath the fluorescent lights of the kitchen was a warm glow. Her skin looked soft and very touchable. He wondered how old she was. He wondered, briefly, what it would be like to touch her face. He stopped himself before he wondered any more. It had been too long since he'd been with a woman like her. Or had he ever? He didn't even want to consider the possibilities.

"He just talks about me to keep from thinking about his mother. To fill up the space."

"There's more to it than that. I can tell."

"Yeah?" he asked softly, unsure.

"Yeah."

He cleared his throat. "Well, I guess tomorrow sometime—whenever I can get away from work—I'll go to the police and file a missing person's report."

"I'll start checking with all the missions. He may have decided it was too cold to remain on the streets. He may have tried to get in one of the shelters."

Mark stared at her. "You don't really believe all that nonsense about Pop wanting to live under a bridge."

"I'm not sure it's nonsense."

"Oh, come now, Miss Johnson. Get serious. Why would he want to do that?"

"Maybe to assert his independence. Maybe to get your attention. I don't know for sure."

"My attention! Well, he has definitely done that. What is this? The man is eighty-two years old. He's not a kid. He's my father. What does he need my attention for?"

"Old people are often like children, Mark. They need to feel loved. They want to feel needed."

"It's not easy living with your father."

"Oh, you don't have to convince me of that," she said. "I can well imagine. But Spencer loves him very much."

Mark sighed. "I know that. I wasn't trying to run him off. I mean not really. I was just making a suggestion that he could maybe think about a retirement home. The brochure I gave him was for a really nice one. It costs a small fortune to live there."

"How did you hear about it?"

"Abel—my father-in-law—told me about it."

"So one grandfather is suggesting that you put the other grandfather in a home."

Mark's jaw snapped. "You don't understand."

"You're right. I don't understand that."

Mark stood and carried his cup to the sink. Leah followed with hers and removed the pan of milk from the stove.

"I'll get these," said Mark.

"No, no. I said I'd do them."

"You don't have to."

"I know."

"I'll do them."

"No, I'll—"

They stood inches apart, vying for position at the sink, until the silliness of the whole situation took hold.

Mark stepped back a bit, aware of an electric current that pulsated between them. It was crazy. This wasn't supposed to happen. "This is ridiculous," he said. "Fighting over dishes."

Leah felt the current, too, but she laughed to keep it light. "I'm afraid we've gotten off on the wrong foot with each other. I just wanted to help."

He watched her brush the hair from her face with her fingers. "Why?"

She shrugged. "I don't know. I like to help people. I liked Spencer the minute I met him. I hate the thought of his grandfather wandering the streets without a home."

Mark noticed that she didn't say anything about liking him. But that was okay. It was better that way. And he wasn't so sure he liked her, either. "I'll find him."

"I know. I would just like to help." The room was warm and filled with something sharp and bright. She wished she hadn't come tonight. It had been a big mistake. "For Spencer," she managed to say. "It'll be my Christmas present to him."

Mark wished he knew what he was feeling. He wanted her out of his house. So why did he have this need to ask her to stay? "All right," he said. "I probably could use some help. There's so much going on at work right now. I just don't seem to have any time."

"I'll take his picture with me tomorrow and I'll check at all the missions. Somebody is bound to have seen him. It's a start, anyway."

"I—I appreciate it, Miss Johnson. Really. I've probably been kind of rude, but there's just—I don't know, I guess there's too much on my mind right now."

"That's okay," she said. "But please, call me Leah."

Mark had never had trouble relating to women. In fact, they had always made it easy for him. This one was making it easy now. But in a different way. She was approaching him as a friend, something new for him. And there was something about her that was above and beyond the level of sophistication he was used to in women. She was relaxed and easy and straightforward. Like the people he had grown up with. Like the ones he had spent his life running from. To come to her level would be a step backward. Still, there was something about her...

"I'll do these dishes," he said. "You've got a bit of a drive ahead of you. And the roads might be icy."

"Oh, I didn't drive. I don't have a car."

"How did you get here, then?"

"I took the bus."

He stared at her as if she had just arrived from Mars. "You're kidding!"

She laughed. "No. I'm not kidding."

He couldn't believe it. She came all the way over here on a bus just to get a picture of Pop. Just so she could help.

"Don't look so stunned, Mark. The bus isn't so bad."

"But at night."

She shrugged.

He wiped his hands on a towel. "I'll take you home, then."

"Goodness, no," she said. "I came on the bus. I can go home on the bus."

"No way. I'm not going to let you do that."

Standing in front of him, she planted her hands on her waist and blocked his path. "Look, Spencer has gone up to bed. I'll be fine. I do this all the time."

She was so close. Too close. The room was closing in on him. "I'll get him up."

She shook her head. "Please, let me just go home the way I came."

Doubt wavered in his mind.

"Look at me," she laughed, lifting a booted foot from the floor. "I look like a mercenary. I'd scare anybody off."

You look great, he wanted to say. You're the best thing I've seen all day. But the words wouldn't come. Once again, he wished he could know what it was like to touch Leah Johnson. Just to see what she felt like. Just to satisfy his curiosity. Just to know.

She was already heading for the entryway. "I'm going to walk you to the bus stop," he said.

She stopped at the door and slipped into her coat. "Okay."

He took off his suit coat, grabbed a leather jacket from the closet and slipped it on.

When the door opened, a blast of wintry air was sucked into the foyer. The chill sent a sharp ache to Mark's bones. "Pop," he mumbled softly, thinking of his absentminded father sitting cold and hungry under a bridge somewhere.

Leah lightly touched his arm. "He'll be fine. We'll find him tomorrow. Don't worry."

Her hand was gone from his arm as quickly as it landed there. He was not prepared for her. They began the short walk to the bus stop. "I just can't believe he did this," Mark said into the wind. "What a foolish thing to do."

"Sometimes we do that," she said. "Sometimes we run away from the very place where we ought to stay. Human nature, I guess. Oh, here comes the bus. I'll start looking tomorrow. Tell Spencer not to worry."

The bus pulled up and the door slid open. Mark didn't want her to go, but he knew there was really no reason for her to stay. If he could think of something else to ask her, something more to say...

"Good night, Mark," she said. "Sleep well."

"Good night—"

She stepped into the bus and the door slid closed.

"—Leah," he said too late.

Chapter Six

The night was bitterly cold. The wind howled around the corners of buildings and swept down alleyways walled by stone and brick. Out of need, Pop Carruthers joined the five men and two women around the fire burning in the trash can. The others were reluctant at first to allow him near, which made him think of the squawking territorial disputes the chickens used to have behind the house on Lindy Creek. This alley belonged to them. He was the outsider. The uninvited. But they knew what it was to be cold and alone, so he was allowed to stay.

Warming his hands over the fire, his eyes flitted from one face to the other. The expressions were pretty much the same. Ambiguous and listless, with eyes that were fixed on another place and time, and with features that were all bones and sharp angles. They lived for the moment of warmth, for the few precious seconds of relief. Their minds appeared dazed, with no hopes for tomorrow. All that stretched before them was a cold, bleak expanse of dark followed by light then more dark.

Pop was homesick. He longed for the rolling gray hills of Blue Mountain, for family and friends sitting around hot iron stoves, cooking hoecakes and sharing gossip. He remembered how on cold days the relatives would come running out of the piney woods and hightail it down to his house. Ellie would always cook up enough corn bread for a Bible story then use the opportunity to collect money for one of the neighbors in need. She had an old pickle jar that she'd set out on the table, and when Cus'n Bull's tractor needed a new belt or when Aunt Jo's and Uncle Rud's barn burned up, Ellie'd expect her guests to fill up the pickle jar with plenty of charitable contributions.

The woman warming her hands beside Pop edged a little closer, seeking human warmth. He reached out and slipped an arm around her, thinking of Ellie. It was easy to forget that some days were gone forever, that loved ones and friends had gone away and left him behind. It seemed like just yesterday that spring was bounding over the hillsides like a new pup; that Ellie, looking as pretty as a new sunrise, was out filling her basket with wild dewberries; that Mark, all scrawny limbs and unwashed neck, was running barefoot through the clover, chasing a fat rabbit into a smoking log.

The woman beside Pop mumbled something, and when he looked down, he saw that she was grinning through dark teeth and holding up a bottle of Boone's Farm. He brought his arm to his side and shivered inside his woolen coat.

He sure was homesick. Getting to know the city wasn't as much fun as he'd figured it would be. He missed Spencer. Right now, they'd probably be whupping up something to eat. Sody crackers with mayonnaise sure sounded good about now. Maybe tomorrow, he'd head up to the mountain. He'd told Spencer that he wasn't going to Cus'n Cooter's, but the fella's old place would be a heck of a lot warmer than this. He could at least have him some hot vittles and good talk. Maybe that's what he'd do. He'd take what money he had left in his pocket and go buy Cooter a present. Then he'd head on up for a surprise visit.

Suppressing another chill, Pop reached over and took the offered drink from the woman. He tipped back the bottle and took a big swig. It went down his throat some good.

THE PHONE WAS RINGING when Leah unlocked the front door, stepped inside her living room and closed and locked the door behind her. She dashed into the kitchen and grabbed the receiver.

"Hello."

"Miss Johnson?"

Her heart began an erratic beat inside her chest. *Miss Johnson*. So he was still insisting on that level, was he? "Is that you, Mark?"

"Yes." He paused, wishing he hadn't called. Wanting to kick himself for the folly of it all. "I just wanted to make sure you got home all right."

"Yes, I just walked in when the phone was ringing."

"Oh."

"That's very sweet of you to call and check on me."

Sweet. God, how idiotic she must think he was for worrying. But he had been, and it really bugged him that he had. "I just don't need that on my conscience, too," he said too brusquely.

"What do you mean?"

"I mean I've got enough things to feel guilty about. If anything had happened to you on the way home, that would have just been one more layer."

"How nicely put," she said dryly. "I'm certainly glad I didn't die on the way home and burden you with more problems."

"I didn't mean it that way."

"Well, you don't have to worry about me. I have no intention of being a burden on anyone."

"Oh, that's right. You're too busy taking on everyone else's burdens. Are you one of those who believes the world can be a perfect place?"

"Did you call to insult me, Mark?"

Damn! Why couldn't he get anything right lately? Why did he have this need to lash out at everyone around him? And that wasn't why he had called. He *had* been worried about her taking the bus home. And there was something else, but he didn't want to think about that right now. He didn't have room in his life to think about anything else.

"No," he said quietly. "I—I just wanted to make sure you were all right."

She heard it. She heard something in his voice that made her sad and scared and excited all at the same time. She wanted to fix Mark Carruthers, but for Spencer's sake. She wanted to bring a joyful Christmas to a lonely little boy. That was all. She didn't want a permanent fixer-upper in her life. And she certainly didn't want to admit that maybe, just maybe, she had a few needs of her own.

"Thank you for calling, Mark. I'll—I'll let you know if I find out anything about your father."

"Okay." He racked his brain for something else to say, for an excuse to keep her on the line. Even though Spencer was asleep down the hall, the big house was awfully empty. His bedroom was cold and big and empty. And his bed was too big. Too empty. He remembered the tumultuous junk that filled her house and he wondered if her bedroom looked the same. Chaos, tumult, warmth. He could think of nothing to say.

"Thank you, Leah."

He said it. He said her name. And the sound of it came not from the disciplined, polished man she had seen tonight. The voice was rough and unrestrained, coming from some lawless place within him that he had not been able to control.

Leah put the receiver in its cradle and leaned against the counter, breathless. Where had that come from? Who was Mark Carruthers, and what was buried deep inside him that he was afraid people would see? She had glimpsed it earlier tonight, this hidden self, this other man.

She could easily handle the troubles of a handsome, cool sophisticate who held dinner parties and made deals with four-star generals. But she wasn't at all sure she could handle the problems of a devastatingly good-looking single father who had an untamed, seething man lurking beneath the skin.

She wanted to help them, but she certainly didn't want to come to the point where she might need them, too. Leah Johnson needed no one. She knew, only too well, how if you needed someone, they twisted that need to suit themselves. She had given all of herself that she could. She couldn't afford the hurt.

Don't make me care for you, Mark Carruthers. Please don't make me care.

MARK LAY BACK against his pillow and folded his hands behind his head. He stared at the ceiling. Before his eyes was an image of Leah Johnson, propped up in a small iron bed with a notepad in her lap. She was writing furiously, making lists, taking notes, cataloguing all the things she had to do, keeping track of all the projects she had to complete. Around her was a room crammed full of embroidered pillows with lace doilies covering cast-off furniture. The pen was scratching across the paper in fast, furious strokes. In his mind, he saw himself reach out and take the pen from her hand. Pulling her down into the bed, the strokes of his hands replaced all need for lists or commitments or other people.

Reaching to switch out the light on his bedside table, Mark took a deep breath and forced himself to think about Abel's plans for him for tomorrow. And the next day. And the next.

THE BELL ABOVE THE DOOR of the DeHaven Center tinkled, and Lilla DeHaven glanced up from the rack where she was organizing men's ties. It took a moment for her to focus on who was standing inside her store, a cane looped over his wrist.

"Why, Delbert Carruthers." She beamed. "How on earth are y'?"

Pop strolled over to the rack where Lilla stood, and grasped her around the waist. He tried to pick her up, but he'd either forgotten how heavy she was or how weak he had grown.

"Now, don't you go and do that, Carruthers. You'll break your back. I've gained a few pounds since the last time you saw me and—well, you're certainly no spring chicken.''

He slapped her soundly on the behind. "And you're as sassy as ever, I see.''

She laughed good-naturedly. "That's the only way I can keep old coots like you at a distance.''

"Y' mean to tell me, Lilla, that nobody's dragged y' to the altar yet?''

"Heavens to Betsy, no! The altar and the coffin are two places I won't go willin'.''

"Plan on kicking and screaming to the end, do y'?''

"I most certaintudily do. Now, why don't y' come over here and have some of my little cakes. I baked 'em fresh 'smorning and I can't seem to give 'em away.''

They walked across the store, and Pop looked at the table full of food. "What is it?''

"It's my Russian Communist tea cakes. It is some good, but I can't seem to get rid of 'em. There's so many of them out-of-work Yankee Communists moving into town every day, I thought for sure they'd come in and eat it up. And you remember these, don't y', Carruthers? These are ice-box cookies, made from Sally Beaudette's recipe.''

"Miss Beaudette's ice-box cookies!" Pop picked up one and popped it in his mouth. His eyes closed as pleasure took over.

"Don't it just make y' wanna lay down and scream?"

He swooned. "I feel like I'm back huntin' coon with Elbert and we've stopped by that little crick that runs near the Beaudettes'. Miss Sally'd always come running out of the trees at us with a handful of her cookies wrapped in paper. Never said nothin'. Just handed us the cookies, then took off like Ady's goose into the woods again."

"She never was quite right," agreed Lilla. "Some disease she had when she was a baby. They said it eat up part of her brain."

"She shore could make the best ice-box cookies, though."

Pop ate another and they stood together, silently remembering good times past.

Pop grinned at the short, stout woman beside him. "It shore is good to see y', Lilla."

She slapped him on the arm. "Aw, you're just saying that."

"I mean it." He leaned down and kissed her plump cheek.

Lilla gathered herself up into her best imperious stance. "Don't get all moony-faced now, Carruthers," she said. "You're too old to come courtin' a woman my age."

"I'm in the prime of my life," argued Pop.

"Well, y' look like hell. Where y' been keeping yourself anyways?"

"I've been staying over to my son's."

Lilla studied the unshaven face, the uncombed hair and the dirty pants. "Uh-huh." She picked up the plate of cookies and held them away from him. "You're lying through your eyeteeth, Delbert Carruthers. Now, are y' gonna tell me where you been holin' up, or am I gonna have to deprive y' of Miss Beaudette's ice-box cookies?"

"I'm telling y'. I've been staying with Mark. You 'member my boy, Mark. He's got hisself a fancy house over on the west side of town. I been staying over there for the past year or so. Till last night."

"Where were you last night?"

"I took off."

"What do y' mean, y' took off?"

"I just plum took off, that's what I mean. Mark dudn't want me stayin' there no more."

"Oh, pshaw!" said Lilla, setting the plate of cookies on the table. "I don't believe that for a minute. I know that boy of yours. He was always a little bit rowdy, but good. Real smart, too. Y' must be wrong."

Pop shook his head. "Nope. He wants me to go live in one of them retirement homes. Said it straight out to my face."

Lilla took in air and breathed out slowly. "Land's sake," she said softly.

"It's the gospel truth," he declared, raising his right hand.

"Where'd y' go last night?"

"I just kinda hung out on the streets. Met me a bunch of pretty decent folk. City folk, though, not country. Out of work, most of 'em."

"I know," she said, shaking her head. "I see 'em in here every day. Too many people, not enough jobs to go around. What are y' going to do?"

"You 'member Cooter Johns?"

"Lawd, I haven't seen him in ages. You mean to tell me he's still alive?"

"Last I heard," said Pop, realizing for the first time that it was possible he wasn't. He sure hoped Cooter hadn't up and died on him before he could even go for his surprise visit.

"So that's where you're goin'?"

"Thought I might. But I wanted to get him a little somethin' to take."

"Like what?"

"I don't know. Clothes or something."

"Pshaw! Cooter Johns hasn't put on clean clothes for the last thirty years. I'll bet the ones he's wearing are stuck to his skin."

"Well, a hat then."

She nodded. "I got hats. Come on over here." She led him to a long table stacked three high in hats. "This felt one's right nice. Good enough for the likes of Cooter."

Pop took a look. "Not bad. How much?"

She flipped over the tag attached to the brim. "Seventy-five."

Pop reached into his pocket and pulled out three quarters.

"Now let's do this right," she said, marching over to the checkout counter. "I've got procedures, Carruthers. I don't want y' comin' in here and gummin' up my works."

She took a piece of carbon paper and carefully placed it between two sheets in her receipt book. She wrote, "One felt hat, sold to D. Carruthers as gift for Cooter Johns. Seventy-five cents ($.75)." She added the date and the time, then tore off the top copy and handed it to Pop. "Now I'll take the money."

Pop handed it over and watched Lilla open the cash drawer and drop it in. He grinned at her and couldn't resist another kiss on her cheek.

"Oh, pshaw," she said.

LEAH FINISHED SEWING a patch on a used pair of boy's Levi's, then folded them and placed them on the stack with the other jeans. "It's really sad," she was saying. "This little boy misses his grandfather so much."

"And the boy's daddy?" asked Lilla from her perch behind the counter where she was tallying up the receipts in her notebook.

Leah evened out her breathing. The boy's daddy. What about him, Leah? She had stayed awake for hours last night, tossing and turning, remembering his voice when he said her name over the phone. Remembering his eyes, so blue and serious and sad. Thinking about his shoulders and arms and hands, strong and powerful, revealing a past that he was determined to hide.

She had lain awake wishing for things that could not be, haunted by sensations she had not felt in a long time. She didn't want to feel them now. They signified hurt just around the corner.

"I don't know," she said quietly. "I can't figure him out. He's a real puzzle. I get the feeling he doesn't really know what he wants."

"Well, I'm shore it will all turn out right in the end. Maybe y' oughtn't get too involved in this one." She looked at Leah, then shook her head with a laugh. "Never mind. I might as well be talking to a brick wall."

Leah smiled. "Well, you know me. I've never been one to sit on the sidelines."

"How are y' goin' to go about finding him?"

"I checked some of the missions this morning. Showed his picture around to see if anybody had seen him."

"And?"

Leah shook her head. "Nobody had." She brightened. "But I'll just have to keep looking, won't I?"

"Reckon so," said Lilla, closing her notebook. "Why don't y' let me take a peek at the picture, and if he should happen by here, I can let y' know."

Leah went into the back room and pulled the photograph from the big canvas bag she carried around. She brought it out and showed it to Lilla.

"Land's sake," said Lilla softly. She looked at Leah. "This is the old man you're lookin' for?"

"Yes."

Lilla took the picture into her own hands and stared at it.

"What is it, Lilla? Do you know him? Pop Carruthers is his name."

"Gracious sakes alive," she murmured. "Delbert."

"Delbert?"

"That's his name. Delbert Carruthers." She looked up from the picture and said to Leah, "He was in here this morning."

"In the center?"

"Yep. Picking out a hat for Cooter Johns."

"What do you mean?"

"I mean he was buying a hat for his Cus'n Cooter, 'cause that's where he was headed."

"Where is that?"

"Back up in the sticks. 'Bout eight or nine miles from here. Up nears Toad's Soup."

"Toad's Soup. Is that a town?"

"Well, it ain't much of one. Just a fillin' station and a grocery."

"I can't believe this, Lilla! What luck. I can't wait to tell Mark and Spencer."

Lilla laid a hand on Leah's arm. "Hold on a second there, girly. Now, maybe he don't want them to know."

"But they're worried about him."

"Yep, I 'magine they are. But he didn't seem too happy with his boy this morning. Said he was wantin' him to go to one of them retirement places."

"I don't think he really wants him to go. Mark just suggested it to him, that's all. I think he realizes it was a big mistake."

"I know that boy," said Lilla. "I just can't figure how he could go and hurt his daddy like that."

"You know Mark?"

"Lawd, yes. He used to come in here when he was no more'n a whisker on his daddy's chin. Wild little thing, he was. I'd be in here helping Mama and the minute she saw them come in, she'd make me drop whatever I was doin' and go keep an eye on that boy. There was no telling what he was like to do, she'd say. I always figured the reason he caused so much mischief was 'cause he was bored. Y' know, he was real smart. They had to send him off to school in Edgeton 'cause he got too smart for LaVinda Bills. She was the teacher up where they lived on Lindy Creek." Lilla frowned. "Never saw him too much after he started coming to school in town, though. I 'member his cus'n, Bobby Sue Wallis, once came in here, and when I asked her about her cus'n Mark, she told me he didn't want to have nothin' to do with none of 'em. Said he'd gotten too good for the likes of 'em. That's what she said.''

Leah didn't want to let images of Mark Carruthers fill her mind. They had taken up enough room last night. But the images came anyway. ''Was he really poor, Lilla?''

''Oh, my, yes. Poor as the dirt in Frydeck Gulch. Old Delbert, well, he cut and sold hay some, but that was seasonal work, y' know. Worked some on the road crews that came through in winter, too, but he never earned enough to make much of a scratch.''

''I can't picture Mark as poor,'' Leah said, as the image of a dark-haired boy running in patched jeans through the DeHaven Center sliced through her mind. She tried to see it and connect it to the serious man who had stood before her last night, dressed in dark gray suit and tie, in the entry hall of his fine home on the west side of town. Was it poverty that had wiped any joy from his life? Was it the long, hard struggle to success that had done it? Was it the desertion by his wife? She fervently wished she didn't care what the answers were, but she did.

And, despite what Lilla said, she felt sure that Mark wanted his father to come home. Mark was worried, and he would want to know where Pop was.

As soon as she could get away from the center, Leah dashed to her house and called Constance Aeronautics. The switchboard operator connected her to Mark's secretary, who informed her that Mr. Carruthers would be in a meeting until late afternoon and would she care to leave a message.

"Just tell him that Leah Johnson called and that I have wonderful news for him."

After she hung up, she called Mark's home. Spencer answered.

"Hi, Leah," he said.

"Hi, Spencer, what's going on?"

"Ah, nothing," he said lethargically. "Just playing Nintendo. It's so boring around here."

She had intended to tell him about Pop. But now that she was talking to him, she had a better idea. "Listen, Spencer, you want to go for a ride?"

"A ride in what?"

"In a car."

"My dad said you don't have a car."

"I'm going to borrow one."

"Where are you going?"

"Well," she said, "how would you like to go with me up to your cousin's house? I think we might just find Pop there."

Spencer nearly dropped the phone. "Really? You mean it? You've found Pop?"

"Well, I think so. The woman I work with said that he told her that he was going to Cooter Johns' house."

"That's Cus'n Cooter," said Spencer. "I never met him, but Grandpa talks about him all the time."

"You want to go with me?"

"Yes!" he cried. "Is Daddy going, too?"

"I can't get hold of him at his office."

"He'll be mad when he finds out where Pop went. He doesn't like the cousins."

"Well, I'm sure he'll just be pleased to find Pop again. Now, I want you to go ask Clara if it's okay for you to go with me."

"Okay." Spencer dropped the phone on the table, and Leah jerked the receiver away from her ear. She could hear him running, then she heard the faint timbre of his voice as he called Clara's name.

After a couple of minutes, he came running back to the phone. "She says it's okay, but I don't think she's real happy that we found Pop."

"I have to round up a car, Spencer, but I'll be over there as quickly as I can. Wear something warm, okay?"

"Okay. Bye." He slammed the phone down.

THE MEETING had been dragging on for what seemed like hours. And, in direct proportion, Mark's attention span had grown shorter. He had gone to the police station this morning and filled out the report on

Pop. Now, they told him, it was a matter of wait and see.

He had never been good at waiting. Waiting never got you ahead in life. He was a man of action, a man who wanted fast results. He wanted to know where Pop was now.

He hadn't heard anything from Leah Johnson. But then, he had been in this meeting for almost two and a half hours. Maybe he should sneak out and give her a call. Or maybe Spencer had heard something.

Fortunately, a break in the meeting was called, and Mark was the first one out of the boardroom.

Once in his office, he dialed Leah's number but got no answer. He tried his home phone. After several rings, Clara answered.

"They're what!" he exploded, when she told him that Leah had come for Spencer in a borrowed car. "What time did they leave?"

"About one-thirty."

Damn. They had been gone two hours already. He'd never be able to catch up with them. And gone to the mountains. She didn't even call and tell him!

He slammed down the phone, and his secretary appeared at his door. "Here are your phone messages, Mr. Carruthers."

A call had come at noon, he saw, looking at the slip of paper his secretary handed him. *Tell him I have great news for him.*

He leaned back in his leather chair and let out a slow breath. Anger was the operative word here, but he wasn't sure at whom it was directed. Was he mad at Leah for being able to find Pop when he couldn't? Was he angry that she took Spencer to the mountains and he was, once again, left out of his son's life?

Or was it that she would have a glimpse of where he had come from and what he was made of? Once she saw it firsthand, he knew he wouldn't have to worry about whether Leah was right for him. The opportunities—the unspoken possibilities—would be quietly withdrawn. Forever.

THOUGH SHE'D HAD NO TROUBLE borrowing a car from a friend, the drive to Toad's Soup took a little longer than Leah had anticipated. The road was rutted and slick in spots, and the numerous bridges were not only icy, but rickety and old. Leah drove slowly and carefully, wishing silently that she hadn't brought Spencer along. He was great company, but she was worried about his safety.

The town of Toad's Soup was hard to miss. It was the only gas station they had seen since leaving Edgeton—a vaguely white wood building with a tin roof and a big sign that read Toad's Exxon. Toad pumped the gas, washed the windshield, sold fishing licences and, if you were in the market, sliced up a side of bacon for you.

"I'm the mayor, the grocer and the gas pumper," Toad told them with a smile. "And I shore do 'preciate yer bidness. Where y' headin' anyways?"

"We're goin' to see my grandpa," said Spencer, staring in at a jar of fat night crawlers Toad displayed on the counter.

"And who'd that be?"

"Delbert Carruthers," said Leah as she paid him for the gas. "He's visiting Cooter Johns."

"Pop Carruthers!" said Toad. He looked at the boy. "He yer granddaddy?"

"Yep, sir," said Spencer.

"Well, I'll be dipped." He looked at Leah. "You know where Cooter stays?"

"No."

"Okay." Toad took her by the arm and led her out in front of the station. "Now then. Y' go down this here road and y' keep goin' till y' pass Helen's place on the left. Y' can't miss her place 'cause it's got a big windmill laying over on its side next to the road. Okay. Now then. Y' go on past her place and you'll cross a little crick. The road goes right after the bridge and then you'll come to a fork. Y' don't want to go right 'cause that'll take y' down to Old Man Jenkins' place down in the bottoms. Y' don't want to go down there 'cause Old Man Jenkins don't take to visitors. Last one down there never come out. And I shore as shootin' ain't goin' down there to find out why not.

"So at the fork, we go left," said Leah, hoping to get on with it. It was already midafternoon and they still hadn't gotten to Cooter's. She had wanted to get Spencer home before his dad got off work, but that now appeared to be out of the question.

"That's right," said Toad. "At the fork, y' go left. Not right."

"No, not right. Left."

"That's right. Left. 'Cause—"

"Old Man Jenkins," cued Leah. "So we want to go left. How far down the road is it then?"

"Well now, it's just spittin' distance from there."

"Oh, good. On the left or the right?"

"Well, now, there ain't no left or right to it. There's just the end of the road. Bessie's Crick runs through there, and it washed out the road so many times, the county just said to hell with it and now it's the end of the road. That's where y'll find Cooter Johns."

"'Preciate it," Leah said, then shook her head. Goodness, she was starting to sound just like him! Spencer grinned at her.

They climbed into the car and drove down the narrow rutted lane, winding in and out of the trees and over more bridges, until they came to the fork.

"Don't go right," Spencer warned.

"I won't," said Leah. They turned left and drove to the end of the road. At one time a dead-end sign had been posted there by the county, but it now lay on its back in the icy mud beside Bessie's Crick.

Leah left the car on the road and she and Spencer got out and closed the doors.

"I hope Cousin Cooter doesn't have a loaded gun nearby."

At that moment a loud pop from a rifle rent the air. Leah jumped back and grabbed Spencer, pulling him behind her.

"Got 'im!" someone called. "Got that ornery critter. Y' see that, Cooter? We're gonna have us some supper after all."

"That's Grandpa!" said Spencer. "He's got him some animal."

Leah relaxed her hold on Spencer and together they walked through the trees toward the house.

"Yoo-hoo," she called, not wanting Pop to think they, too, were ornery critters that needed to be shot. "Mr. Carruthers? Mr. Johns?"

They came into the clearing where the house sat, and the two old men remained still as deer, Pop in the grass holding a rabbit and Cooter half reclining on the porch on a couch with his feet propped on an up-turned washtub. Both men appeared amazed at the intrusion, as if they hadn't heard human voices for years.

"Spenner? Is that you, boy?"

"It's me, Grandpa." He broke free of Leah's hand and went running toward the old man. With a strength that surprised Leah, Pop picked the boy up in a fierce bear hug and swung him around.

"What in tarnation are y' doin' here?" Pop asked when he set Spencer down.

"We came to get you," said Spencer.

Pop looked at Leah. "Who's this?"

Leah stepped forward. "My name's Leah Johnson. I'm a friend of Spencer's."

"She's gonna be my new music teacher, Pop."

"She is? Well, ain't that just dandy." Pop stuck out his hand. "Any friend of Spenner Jake is a friend of mine."

Leah took his hand and smiled. "He's been a bit worried about you."

Pop looked at the boy. "Y' have?"

"Yes, Grandpa. I looked everywhere for you. I thought you were lost, and then I got lost, and then Leah found me, and then she took me to her house, and then Daddy came to get me, and boy, was he mad!"

"Mad at me?"

"And at me," said Spencer.

"And at me," said Leah.

Pop chuckled. "How did you find me?"

"Leah found you."

He looked to her for explanation.

"I work with Lilla DeHaven at the center, and she told me you had come in this morning. She said you were coming up here for a visit, so Spencer and I decided to drive up and visit you."

"You don't aim to drag me back to town, do y'?"

"Not if you don't want to go."

"Well, I don't."

"Okay."

Satisfied with her response, he nodded his approval of her. He laid a callused hand on Spencer's head and smiled. "I shore am glad you're here, though, Spenner boy."

"Me, too, Pop." Spencer hugged his grandfather's waist. "Hey, your barn door's open."

Pop looked down, then zipped up. "Why don't y' come over here and meet Cus'n Cooter."

Pop picked up the rabbit by the hind legs and handed it to Spencer. He took the boy's other hand in his, and they started walking toward the porch. Pop stopped and turned around. "You, too, Johnson. Come on up and set a spell."

Leah followed with a smile. She liked Pop Carruthers. Already she knew he was a person she could respect and really like. He reminded her very much of Spencer. Very open. Very honest. He knew who he was, and he wasn't a bit ashamed of it.

He was very different from Mark.

Cooter didn't say anything as the introductions were given, nor did he move. He did shift his pipe from one side of his mouth to the other, and Leah, who refused to admit that some people could remain strangers, took that as a welcoming sign.

"Cooter, he don't say much," explained Pop.

She smiled. "It sure is a pleasure to meet you, Cooter. I hope you don't mind us barging in on you like this."

"I bought that hat for him," Pop said proudly. "Look's right nice on him, don't it?"

"It sure does."

"Got it at Lilla's place." He turned his appraisal on her. "You really work with her, Johnson?"

"Yes. And I live next door to the center."

"In that house with all the green stuff on the door?"

"Yes, that's my Christmas wreath."

"That shore is pretty. I noticed it right off s'morning. Looks real nice."

"Thank you, Mr. Carruthers."

"Call me Pop. Everbody else does. How long you been working with Lilla?"

"About a year. She owns the house I live in, and I help pay my rent by working for her."

"Fine woman, she is," said Pop, staring out over the litter-strewn yard. "Always did have a special fondness for her."

"Where do I put this rabbit, Pop?" asked Spencer.

"Just set her down over here, boy. We're gonna fry her up for supper. Y' want some?"

"Can we stay for supper, Leah?"

She hated to dampen his enthusiasm, but Mark would kill her if she kept him out late. And she didn't really want to drive down the narrow, icy roads at night.

Pop sensed her hesitation. "Might be a little late when we get her cooked, boy," he said. "Yore daddy might be worried 'bout y'."

Spencer frowned. "He doesn't care."

Pop studied his grandson's scowl and said, "Now we've talked 'bout this before, Spenner. Y' know how much yore daddy loves y'. He's just busy with work and all. He's an engineer," Pop said to Leah, pride written all over his face. "Designs all sorts of fancy jets. You met him?"

"Yes." *Met him and carried him in my sleep.*

He elbowed her side. "What'd y' think of him? Good-lookin' fella, ain't he?"

She felt her face grow warm. "He's, uh, very—"

He wrapped his arm around her. "You married, Johnson?"

"No, sir, I'm not."

"Never been?"

"No, sir."

"How come?"

She laughed nervously. "I—I don't know. I—"

He gave her a big hug and glanced toward the porch. "Y' think I'm too old for her, Cooter?"

"Yep." The washtub scooted an inch along the porch when Cooter readjusted his ankles.

Pop's arm slid from her shoulder. "Well, reckon I am."

He tousled Spencer's hair. "I tell y' what, boy. You can plan to come up here early some mornin' and just stay the whole day. We'll go huntin' together." He looked at Leah. "You, too, Johnson. Y' can come up here and stay the day with us. Right, Cooter?"

"Yep," said Cooter, shifting the pipe once more to the other side of his mouth.

"That would be lots of fun," said Leah. "I'd love it."

"Reckon you could get Mark to come?"

"I'm sure he'd come."

"He wouldn't come," said Spencer.

"He'll come," she said to the boy. She looked at Pop and said with determination, "He'll come."

Chapter Seven

Mark was fuming. "First you drag my son off to God only knows where, then you don't even bring my father home." He turned toward his son. "Go to the kitchen, Spencer, and have Clara fix you something to eat before she leaves."

Spencer took off his cold, wet coat and carried it with him toward the kitchen. "Yes, sir."

Leah was left alone to fend off Mark's wrath. "I called here a hundred times," he said. "I had to keep hearing Clara tell me that you hadn't brought them back. There's a major winter storm brewing out there tonight, do you realize that?"

"I realize," she answered calmly, refusing to be intimidated by him. The drive home had been agonizingly slow. Ice fell against the windshield and froze under the wipers. The roads were slick and dark. She hadn't remembered all those curves from when they went up the mountain in the daylight. "I certainly didn't mean to have Spencer out so late. The time just—kind of got away from us."

"Got away from you."

"Yes. Spencer was having so much fun with Pop that I couldn't bear to tell him it was time to go."

Mark spun away and stalked into the living room. "You shouldn't have taken him in the first place."

Still wearing her coat, Leah followed him into the other room. "Clara gave him permission."

"Well, I didn't."

"I called your office, but you were in a meeting."

Mark sighed and turned toward her. "Look, Leah, I appreciate your help in finding Pop. But I can handle him from here."

This was it, then, she realized. She had fulfilled her little job, and now she was being dismissed.

Summarily.

Her services were no longer needed.

Adios, pal.

"The way you handled him before?" she blurted out, furious more with herself than with him. She asked for it. She laid herself wide open for the hurt.

He glared at her. "Who the hell do you think you are, lady?"

She lifted her chin. "I am Spencer's friend. I am Pop's friend." *I am nothing to you.* The unspoken words came across loud and clear.

He continued to glare at her, furious with himself for letting his temper get the best of him. He had been worried about her as well as Spencer. He had been afraid of her reaction to him now that she knew the stuff he was made of. He had wanted to beat her to the rejection. "Great friend," he smirked. "You don't even bring Pop home."

"He didn't want to come with me."

"Why not?"

"He seemed happy right where he was."

"Happy!" he spat. "Happy staying with that lazy good-for-nothing Cooter?"

"They seemed compatible enough. They were going to cook a rabbit for dinner."

"Look," Mark growled, stepping close to her. "I do not want my father staying in some broken-down shack like poor white trash."

He was only inches away, but Leah lifted her face to meet his squarely. "What makes you say that Cooter Johns is trash?"

"Because he has done nothing with his life. He sits on that porch all day and waits for his government check to come in. He doesn't give a damn about bettering himself."

"So it's the fact that your tax dollars are paying for his laziness. Is that what bugs you so?"

"That's part of it."

"What's the rest?"

"What do you mean?"

"Why else do you resent Cooter and all the other people up there on that mountain so much?"

His eyes darkened. "I don't think that's any of your business."

"You're afraid of them," she said bravely, while inside she felt her courage beginning to wane just a bit.

"Afraid of them?" he scoffed. "Afraid of the likes of Cooter Johns? You've got to be kidding."

"It's what they represent to you, what they remind you of, isn't it? You hated being poor, and you're so ashamed of it that you're trying to erase every reminder of it, aren't you?"

A moment of shock crossed his face, then something else replaced it. Spreading his fingers wide, he grasped both her arms and hauled her up against him. He wasn't going to let her reject him, dammit! He would save her the trouble.

Her breath ceased when his hands wrapped like steel bands around the arms of her coat. His eyes faded into a dark and savage stare.

They stood this way for a long, suspended moment, then his voice came from some harsh place inside him. "You have no idea what it's like to be an outsider all your life. No, you belong everywhere, don't you? You fit in."

Leah shook her head, but he didn't seem to notice. His focus was trained on something beyond her, something he thought only he could see and feel.

"I was poor," he said, never loosening his grip on her arms. "I never fit in with townspeople. I was always an outsider, always the different one, always the hick from the sticks.''

His eyes slid to her mouth then slowly lifted to her brown eyes, watching him with an intensity that burned all the way to the pit of his stomach. His voice lowered. ''You don't know what it's like to want to belong somewhere so badly.''

Something unseen took possession of her, something she had no strength to fight. Her breath grew trapped in the confines of her chest, and she felt the blood pounding in her neck. Mark still held onto her, but there was something different about the grip, something less violent. Something much more threatening.

She opened her lips to speak and noticed that his eyes were trained on her mouth. ''You're wrong, Mark,'' she said softly, with surprising vulnerability. ''You're so wrong.''

One hand loosened and slid up her arm, over her shoulder and onto her neck. The breath left her in a rush. His hand grasped the back of her neck and pulled her even closer.

Her arm free, she lifted it and raised her hand toward him, toward his face, until the flat of her palm lay against his firm jaw. She traced its outline with her fingers and said softly, ''You'd be surprised what I know, Mark.''

His own breath was expelled quickly, and he found it difficult to get enough air. Her soft fingers against his skin were warm and gentle and persuasive. And right now, he didn't need much persuasion. It had been so long since he'd been touched by a woman, so long since he had put himself in this kind of vulnerable position. He didn't want to examine whether he wanted the feeling or not. He knew only that she stirred urges inside him that he had tried to suppress. With his hand, he pushed back her hair and bent down, ever so slowly, and kissed the side of her neck.

Her quick breath landed against his ear, and he felt a growl forming in his mind. His fingers wrapped around a thick strand of hair, and he drew her up tightly against him. His other hand let go of her arm, and he slipped it inside her coat and around her back, holding her captive in his grasp.

"Say it, Leah. Tell me you want nothing to do with me. White trash from Blue Mountain."

He frightened her. He made her want him so desperately. She could see all the hurt that lay ahead, but she could not find the strength to turn away. "This is insane," she said breathlessly. "Please don't make me want you, Mark. I—"

He didn't give her time to question what she was doing. He dipped his head, and his mouth grazed along her chin and over her mouth. Her lips parted in a surprising welcome. He was holding the back of her head tightly, allowing her no room to escape. But she had no intention of trying.

He felt so good to her. She didn't want him to, but he did. His mouth against her mouth, his hand against her back, his fingers in her hair . . .

"Wow!" said a small, surprised voice behind them. "I didn't know you two liked each other."

Mark's hand jerked out of her coat. His fingers let loose her hair. As soon as she was free, they both jumped back, guilty at being caught by an eight-year-old and at allowing themselves to forget the truth that existed between them. The truth that they weren't supposed to like each other.

That he could never expect her to want a man with his past.

That she could never expect anything but hurt from him.

That right now he wanted her more than he had ever wanted anyone.

That, in this moment, she didn't care about the hurt that lay ahead.

That the risk was worth all.

Even now, Leah's body tingled with the raw sensations he had stirred in her. Even now, she wished she were in the circle of his arms with his mouth moving urgently over hers again.

"Does this mean we can all go up and see Pop together?"

Mark dared to glance at Leah. She was looking at the front door as if it would offer her an escape.

"No," he said. "I'm uh, going to go bring Pop home."

"When?" asked Spencer.

Mark looked again at Leah, but she would not face him. "I don't know, son. Soon."

"But, Dad, he promised me I could come up and spend the whole day at Cus'n Cooter's. Leah, too."

Mark let out a ragged breath. "Could we talk about this tomorrow, Spence? You need to get to bed and I—I need to discuss a couple of things with Leah."

"You gonna kiss her again?"

"No," he answered too quickly.

Even the boy wasn't convinced. He started to climb the stairs. "Okay. Good night, Dad."

"Good night, son. I'll be up to tuck you in in a little while."

"'Night, Leah."

She wasn't sure if her voice would work. "Good night, Spencer."

"Thanks for taking me with you today."

She chanced a look at Mark, but he was watching his son. "You're welcome."

Spencer climbed a few more steps, then stopped again. "Hey, Leah, you want to go with me to Santa's Village sometime? Pop and I went, and it's lots of fun. Dad doesn't have time."

"That would be fun," she answered. "You just let me know when you can go."

"Okay. 'Night." He climbed the rest of the stairs and shuffled down the hallway to his room. Mark and Leah stood silent and unmoving until they heard his door close.

It was Leah who spoke first. "I've got to go," she said, knowing that was the last thing she wanted to do but the one thing she absolutely must do.

"Okay," he said quietly, wishing he had the courage to ask her to stay. They still had so much to talk about. She had said things that needed explanation. He realized how little he knew about her. He knew nothing of where she had come from in life or where she was headed. He hadn't really cared. Not until now.

"Would you mind if I went with your son to Santa's Village one of these days?"

He shook his head. "That would be fine." She was standing very still, almost as if she were afraid to move. "Listen, I didn't mean to get so upset earlier," he said. "I was just worried about Spencer. You know, the weather is so—"

"I know. I shouldn't have taken him out in this."

It's okay, he knew he should say. "Well," he said instead, "everyone survived, I guess."

"I guess." She walked to the foyer, avoiding what they both knew they should talk about. Avoiding each other. "Good night, Mark."

He followed and stood beside her as she opened the door. "Are you going to be all right, driving home in this? You can—"

"I'll be fine," she said quickly, before he could ask her to stay.

Why doesn't she look at me and tell me what is happening here? he wondered.

Why doesn't he say something about what happened between us a moment ago? she thought.

"I'm glad we know where Pop is."

"Me, too."

I guess that means I won't be seeing much of him any more.

How am I going to keep her in my life?

"He's really a great guy," she said.

Mark attempted a smile. "Yeah."

She tried to laugh. "A real character."

"He is that."

She turned toward the open door and started to step into the cold, windy night. His hand against the back of her hair stopped her.

"Leah?"

She turned only halfway around.

He cleared his throat, then let out a long sigh. "These things are difficult with a child around."

She looked at him. The unspoken question hung in the air between them. "If you're trying to ask me to stay the night," she said softly, "I won't."

He cleared his throat again. "Okay."

She had to say it. She had to protect herself while she still had the strength. "What happened a while `ago was a mistake, okay?"

Whether it was male pride or something else, Leah didn't know, but she watched his face harden and his eyes grow cool. "Why is that?"

She hesitated, collecting her thoughts, wishing fervently that she could stop her body from feeling the things it felt every time she looked at him. "I like your son, Mark. And I like your father."

"But you don't like me, is that it?"

She glanced at the floor between them. Her voice was barely above a whisper. "Isn't it obvious how I feel?"

He should have known. She wasn't a woman who would give away her affection on a whim. Not Leah Johnson. "Are you afraid of me, Leah?"

I'm terrified, she could have admitted. Instead, she said, "We only met yesterday."

"Yeah," he said. So what?

"You know nothing about me."

"And you know almost everything about me."

"I think I know what you pretend to be. But what and who you really are is another matter."

Something snapped in his jaw. Here it comes. The other shoe was about to fall. "What is that supposed to mean?"

"I think you're running from something. From your past."

His eyes narrowed. That wasn't what he expected. It threw him off guard. But his defenses were already up, his claws out. "Oh? And what about you?"

"What about me?"

"What is it that you're running from?"

"I'm not running from anything."

"Uh-huh. You just go around helping complete strangers every day out of the goodness of your heart, is that it?"

"That's right."

He shook his head. "I don't buy it, lady. Nobody does something for nothing."

"You have a very sour attitude about life, Mark."

"Maybe. But I've known a few bleeding hearts like you. They've all been running from something."

She studied him coolly for a long moment, then stepped onto the front step. "Good night, Mark."

She was the first breath of fresh air he'd had in years. And he was going to let her blow away. There was only one way he could think of to hold on to her. He couldn't let her go. Grabbing her arm, he spun her around to face him. Her chest rose and fell in anticipation of this moment that they both knew they would grasp, even though it could not last. He pulled her against him once more, and his mouth captured hers in a fiery hold that sent heat racing from her head to her toes.

She clung to him because she knew that once he let her go, she would start the emotional plunge.

He released her, slowly, hesitantly. He didn't smile. "Good night, Leah."

"Goodbye, Mark."

Chapter Eight

Sitting at his desk, Mark had a great view to the west where, beyond the city's edge, the flatlands stretched out like an endless sea. There were no mountains in his view, no rolling hills. There was nothing holding him down.

He was trying to work. He had to get this government bid ready for Abel to present by next week. If only he could concentrate. But he couldn't. All he could think about was last night...and Leah. She wasn't the type of woman he wanted in his life. She would never fit into the game plan. And he didn't even think he was drawn to women like her. Money and status obviously held no importance in her life. But there it was—this almost overwhelming need to see her again, to touch her again. She had felt good in his arms. Warm and inviting.

But she had said no more. She had called the whole episode a mistake, not to be repeated. And that was best, really, because they had nothing in common. She annoyed him terribly. She was so...so helpful all the time. She had too much energy for him. She tired him out. Just like Spencer. Just the thought of the two of them—Spencer and Leah—together was enough to make him want to take a nap.

He looked down at the unfinished proposal on his desktop computer screen, then swiveled his chair around and stared out the window. Where always before the view had been reassuring and encouraging to Mark, it was now bleak and cold, an endless stretch of emptiness and loneliness.

Why had he said those things to her last night? Spencer liked her. She had found Pop. She had gone out of her way to help them. And he had repaid her by being rude. It just seemed as if lately he couldn't get anything right. Every relationship was botched...by him.

First he had messed up things royally with Angela. Although the loss of her in his life left no big hole, he still wondered where it was he had gone wrong. Somehow he had failed to become the man she wanted, the man she expected him to be. The day she left, she had called him a provincial peasant. She had told him that he'd never been anything else. That was what hurt the most. Not her leaving, but the truth she left behind.

And then there was Spencer. How was it that Mark could love him so much, but have such trouble showing it? Because he didn't know how to make up for the hurt of Angela leaving, Mark tended to do nothing. And the boy was slipping away from him. He could feel it and see it. They had been so close a few years ago. They had found it easy to hug and kiss and play together. Now he couldn't even remember the last time Spencer had given him a big hug.

Pop had come along and taken his place. And Mark had run Pop off. Sometimes it was simply too hard to love people. Sometimes it was easier not to care.

He turned to the computer and worked for about fifteen minutes on the new design for the military. But he couldn't get it to come out right. It wasn't practical. It wasn't functional. It wasn't cost efficient. It wasn't what he wanted to be doing right now.

He flipped a switch and pushed back his chair. With one last view of the landscape to the west, Mark grabbed his coat and left the office. He stopped only long enough to tell his secretary that he'd be gone for about an hour.

He drove through the west side of town with ease. The streets were all wide and straight and laid out in a logical manner. As he drove east, they became more narrow, like a labyrinthine tunnel that wormed its way to the base of the hills. The buildings were close together and blocked out the sunlight. During the night, the ice had stopped falling, and the streets of downtown were glazed in hard gray patches.

Mark pulled up in front of Leah's house and sat with the engine idling. He had come to apologize for his behavior last night. He had been ungrateful for her help. He had offended her.

He turned off the engine. That was only part of the reason he had come. He couldn't work for thinking about her. He just wanted to see her.

He climbed out of the car and walked up the slick sidewalk to her house. More patiently than last time, he searched through the garland for the doorbell and found it. But no sound came from it. It was obviously broken, and she hadn't bothered to fix it. Somehow that didn't surprise him. Fixing people was Leah's specialty; not fixing things.

He knocked several times until he finally had to accept the fact that she wasn't home. The house was quiet and still.

He hadn't counted on her not being there. He had it all worked out in his mind so well, and he had been rehearsing his speech to her all the way from the office.

Glancing next door at the DeHaven Center, he hesitated. He had promised himself he would never go back there. He would never subject himself to that again. But Leah worked there. She might be there even now. Did he want to see her badly enough to break his promise to himself?

His feet moved slowly, hesitantly, down her front stoop and along the uneven sidewalk to the center. He was several yards from the front door. All he'd have to do was turn and go to the car. He could call her or come by tonight. He didn't really have to do it now.

He shivered inside his coat. Maybe he'd just go into the center for a minute to get warm. He walked to the door and cringed when the bell clanged loudly as the door opened. He remembered vividly the eyes that would turn on him as a child when he walked through that door. Mrs. DeHaven would purse her lips and, with a decisive nod, sic her eldest daughter on him. He wondered who they would sic on him today.

"Land's sake," he heard from across the room. His eyes scanned the large room that looked unchanged from twenty years before and lighted on a heavyset woman who was lining up shoes as if a military inspection was due any minute. But she had stopped straightening and was staring at him. He stared back.

Walking up to him, she narrowed her gaze. "Why, you're the Carruthers boy. I do believe you are."

Something crumbled inside him. After all the years, he was still recognized. Bumpkin was still written all over him. "And you're the DeHaven girl," he said.

She laughed. "I ain't no girl no more. You can call me Lilla."

He didn't want to call her anything. He wanted to turn and run as fast as he could away from her and this place, but his feet were rooted to the spot.

A kind of lethargy set in. "Are you going to follow me around like you always did?"

She laughed again. "I reckon you've growed up a bit. Don't figure you'll go running around the tables and messing up my stacks. Will y'?"

"No, ma'am."

"Well, come on in then and have some of my cakes." She led the way to the table in the corner. "Your daddy was just in here yesterday, eating up all my food and wasting my time."

"Pop was in here?" So that was how Leah had known. He hadn't even bothered to ask her how she found out Pop had gone to Cooter's. He had been too filled first with anger and then with the feel of her in his arms.

"Why, shore. I thought that's why you were here now. Wanted to find him or somethin'."

"No, I already know he went up to see Cooter Johns."

"So the girl told y', did she?"

"Who?"

"Leah."

"Oh, yes. Yes, she did. Actually, that's why I'm here. I wanted to talk to her and—well, I thought she worked here."

"She does sometimes. But she does lots of other things, too. Let's see, today's Wednesday, ain't it?" She squinted her eyes to see the big calendar hanging on the wall behind the checkout counter.

"Yes, ma'am," said Mark.

She continued to squint, not trusting his answer. "Yep," she finally said. "Wednesday. That means she's over to the church. Choir practice this afternoon."

"She sings in a choir?"

Lilla looked at him as if he were daft. "She directs the choir. She's music director over at the Eastside Congregational."

"I didn't know that," he murmured, embarrassed at how little he knew about her. He had kissed her and held her in his arms, and he had trusted her with his son on two occasions, but he didn't even know what she did with her life. He had assumed the DeHaven Center was pretty much it. "Where is that?"

"Over on Elkhorn Avenue. About the four hundred block, I think. Aren't y' gonna eat some of this here cake?"

He looked at the table piled with cookies and cakes and snacks. It made him think of his mother and how she always had the kitchen counter loaded with food. She had loved to cook. Good food and good gossip had made up his mother's life. He hardly remembered a time when she wasn't happy.

"Thanks," he said and picked up a square of yellow cake with gooey frosting on top. "This reminds me of one Mom used to make."

Lilla beamed. "That's her recipe, you ninny. Ellie Carruthers made the best pickle cake in the whole county."

Mark closed his eyes as the taste rolled over his tongue. Memories came flooding back to him and, this time, he didn't push them away. He was maybe ten years old, sitting on the rotten steps of the back porch, watching two pigs tussle with a greasy rag in the yard. He was feeling down about something, but he couldn't remember what. And there was his mother, handing him a piece of pickle cake and a glass of buttermilk, a surefire remedy to cure any sort of blues a boy might have.

He finished the cake while Lilla watched, then he handed her the empty plate.

"It's mighty fine to see you again, Mark. I hear y' got a fine job with some big company."

He shrugged modestly. "It's a good job."

"And y' got y' a boy, too, I hear."

"Yes, Spencer is eight."

"Well, that's fine. Delbert, he was talking all about y' yesterday. He's right proud of y'."

Mark swallowed a lump of self-loathing that was crawling into his throat. "I, uh, did he say how long he was planning to stay with Cooter?"

Lilla shook her head. "Not that I recall."

Mark could tell by the way she was looking at him that Pop had told her about the retirement home. He didn't need to hear words to feel chastised by Lilla DeHaven. Her look said it all.

"Well," he said. "I guess I'll go over to the East-side Congregational, then, and, uh, try to find Leah."

"She'll be there. Right in the sanctuary's where I'd look."

"Okay." He turned toward the door.

"You gonna be comin' back here anytime soon?"

"Oh, well, I don't know."

Lilla walked to her row of shoes. "Well, y' try not to be a stranger now. You can come on back any-time." She grinned at him. "And I won't follow y' around."

He smiled, too. "That's a relief. Thanks for the cake."

"Anytime."

Mark stepped onto the cold sidewalk and let out a long, slow breath. He took in several more and walked toward the car. He had done it. He had gone into the DeHaven Center. He had been recognized. He had talked to Lilla DeHaven. And he had sur-vived. Somehow it hadn't been as painful as he had expected.

Once the car engine was going, he turned on the heater and started driving toward Elkhorn Avenue. The streets were laid out all wrong, so he had to dou-ble back several times until he found his way. About half way down the four hundred block was the East-side Congregational, an old church that someone had recently given a face-lift. It was white with colorful stained-glass windows and a carved wooden front door.

He sat for a minute in the car before getting out. This was another thing he had not done for a very long time. He had not been inside a church since his mother's funeral twelve years ago. He wasn't sure he would be any more welcome here than in the De-Haven Center.

Making his decision to go inside, he locked the car and walked up the short front walkway. Even from here he could hear the choir singing. The sound beckoned him up the sidewalk.

He climbed the big wide steps and opened one of the double front doors. The vestibule was dark and warm, and it took several seconds for his eyes to adjust to the low light. The choir was singing the refrain from the "Hallelujah Chorus" as he walked quietly down the center aisle and took a seat in one of the pews.

Up in front the choir faced him. Leah stood a little to the right with her back toward him. She was wearing baggy fatigue pants and an oversize sweater. If he hadn't held her last night, he wouldn't have known that a slim, firm woman lay beneath all the mounds of clothes.

Her hair was loosely bound at the nape of her neck with a ribbon and, even from where he sat, he could tell she had on no makeup. Still, there was something so beautiful about her. So fresh and real. He hadn't wanted anything real for so long that he now found it difficult to fully comprehend his attraction for her.

The sounds filled the small church, and he couldn't remember when any music had sounded so soothing and good. Time slipped by him and he forgot all about work and about designs and about Abel's pet projects. Nothing, it seemed, could touch him. Nothing hurt.

When the music ended, Leah walked over to the organist with her sheet of music and said, "David, right in here, slow it down a bit. I know you're playing it the way it was written, but the sopranos sound like chipmunks, they're singing so fast."

Everyone laughed, then Leah turned to the choir. "This really sounds great, you guys. I think we'll only need one more practice on Friday night and that will be it. And let's all promise to do it right on Friday, so that Charlie here can make his date."

The laughter circulated once again through the choir loft as everyone gathered up music and filed down from the loft.

"See you on Friday at six," called Leah. "Sounds great, doesn't it, David?"

"It really does." He played through a few more bars then turned off the organ and gathered his pile of music. "How about dinner?" he asked, coming over to where she was picking up her stuff.

"Oh, thanks, David, but I think I'm going to have a quiet evening at home tonight."

He shrugged. "Maybe some other time?" he asked hopefully.

She smiled at him. "Sure. That would be nice."

From where he sat in the pew, Mark could see the disappointment on the man's face. But he couldn't help but feel a kind of elation that Leah had turned David down. Mark would have felt like an idiot if she'd walked off with the organist and left him sitting in an empty church alone.

David and Leah talked for a couple more minutes then started up the aisle together. David saw Mark first and smiled. "We hope we'll have it together by Sunday," he said.

Leah glanced over, surprise filling her face.

"It sounded very nice," said Mark. "Hello, Leah."

She stopped beside the pew. "Hello, Mark. Wh-what are you doing here?"

He glanced at the organist then back to Leah. "Just needed to talk to you."

David took the hint. "Listen, Leah, I'll see you on Friday, okay?"

She lightly touched his arm and said, "Okay, Dave, see you then."

The wind outside pressed against the front doors and they sucked closed solidly. Leah stayed where she was, standing in the aisle with her arms around her music books. A protective, closed stance, he thought.

"Can we talk?" he asked.

She didn't move. "If last night is any kind of basis, then I'd have to say no."

He let out a slow breath. "I came to apologize, Leah."

For what? she wondered. For the kiss or for what he said? "Okay," she said.

"I was out of line."

Again, she wondered about which incident he was referring to. He had said some things that were not kind, but she could easily forgive him for that. He had been worried and angry and confused. It was the other thing—the way she had thrown herself into his embrace with total abandonment—that she had trouble forgiving. He had made her need him. She didn't want to need him or anyone else. He had brought that out of the hidden depths within her, and it frightened her.

"Say something," he said with a half smile. "I feel like an idiot."

She eased into the pew and sat beside him, leaving several feet between them. "How's Spencer?"

"He was fine when I left for work this morning."

"Haven't heard anything from Pop, I guess."

"No. Listen, Leah, could we talk about us, please?"

She set the music in her lap. "I don't know that there is a whole lot to say."

"I think there is," he said. "For starters, I didn't know you were music director of a church. I—I didn't think to ask what you did for a living."

"Now you know."

"You're not making this any easier for me."

"Look, Mark, you said I was a bleeding heart and I was running from something. Maybe so, but this is what I do, and it makes me happy."

"I think that's great, but—if you run from something, don't run from me."

A tingling sensation spiraled from her fingertips, up her arms and into her neck. "I'm not running from you, Mark."

"I think you are."

She looked across the sanctuary as if searching for an escape.

"The choir sounded great. You're very talented."

"Thank you."

"And I'm glad it makes you happy, Leah, but I— well, what if someone other than, say, some charity case or church choir could make you happy? You know, in a more personal way."

"Men have promised me happiness before," she said softly. "I'm really not in the market."

"Not in the market?" Mark shook his head in disbelief. "Lady, I'm not looking for a side of beef."

She stared at him pointedly. "Then what are you looking for?"

He looked away, his eyes sweeping over the sanctuary before they came to rest on her face. "I don't know," he said in a low, even voice. "I guess I just want to get to know you. I don't know why." He frowned, confused by the twisted strains that ran through his mind. She wasn't his type, he kept saying. Abel would never put his stamp of approval on a woman who wore army fatigues to work. It didn't make sense. She didn't exactly represent the life he had run from, but neither did she epitomize the life he had been seeking for so many years. Where did she fit? And why did he care to know her?

She regarded him for a long moment, wishing he wasn't so handsome, wishing she didn't care what troubled him, wishing she didn't want to get to know him, too. If she could keep it light—if she could focus on his family's needs instead of her own . . . That was the key. She forced a friendly, noncommittal smile. "You're a mess, Mark Carruthers. Did you know that?"

He grinned and shrugged.

"What am I going to do with you?"

He pulled the music books from her arms and took her hand. His fingers, roughened by calluses that would never go away, slid over her palm. "Take me on as one of your charity cases, I guess."

It was just a taste, she knew. Those fingers were just a hint of what he could offer her in a physical way. "Aren't you supposed to be at work, Mark?"

He glanced at his watch, then looked at her in startled confusion. "Is it really five o'clock?"

She twisted her arm to check her watch. He didn't let go of her hand. "It is."

"I can't believe it. I can't believe I've been away from work so long. I told my secretary I'd be gone about an hour."

"What time did you leave?"

"About one."

Where have you been? would have been a logical next question, but she didn't want him to think it mattered much to her.

He seemed, however, to hear the question even though it was not asked. "I went by your house, and you weren't there. Then I went to the DeHaven Center and—"

"You did?"

"Yes." He frowned. "Why?"

"I—I don't know. I'm just surprised, that's all."

He knew why she was surprised. She'd heard Spencer say that he hated the cousins. She'd seen firsthand how much he had altered his life since those days on the mountain. She knew him, and that was what surprised him the most. No one had ever bothered to understand the man beneath the shell.

"Lilla DeHaven told me where I could find you."

A sense of wonderment crept over her. He came all the way over here to talk to her. Left work and came to the church to see her. No one had done that before. *Okay, Leah,* she warned. *Get a grip on yourself. Don't enjoy this too much. Don't start expecting it. That's when trouble starts.*

She let his hand slide away from hers. "Mark? Maybe this Sunday, you'd like to bring Spencer to church here."

He shifted on the hard pew. "I—I don't go to church, Leah. I don't have any—well, any real strong beliefs."

"That's okay," she said. "You can come and listen to the choir sing, and you can soak up the sunlight that pours through the stained-glass windows. See," she said, pointing, "even on a cloudy day like today, see how pretty they are?"

Mark studied the windows and thought how pleasurable it was to enjoy something so simple as light through a window. That was what it was about her that intrigued him so. Leah Johnson got such pleasure out of such simple things.

He smiled at her. "Seems like kind of a hedonistic thing to do, though."

"Listen," she said, looking down at her hand, making him wish he were still holding it in his. "I personally feel that people who have strong convictions close themselves up so they can't hear if God's talking to them or not. If you're quiet and open and fairly vague about things, then you're more receptive to hear what God has to say to you." She shrugged. "That's just my own personal philosophy."

Mark stared at her for a long moment, drinking in the soft, natural beauty of her face. He suddenly felt as if years had been lifted from him, as if he were lying buck naked on a warm summer day in the shallow waters of Lindy Creek, watching the birds soar above him while the day drifted by like a dry leaf on an air current.

He was very glad he had come to see her today. It had been a long time since he had felt so good about himself. Or about anyone else.

"I'd ask you out to dinner," he said, "but you told the organist you wanted a quiet night at home."

"Yes."

"I don't suppose I could change your mind."

Yes, she thought helplessly. *You already have.* "Well..."

"We could go by the house and pick up Spencer and we could go get a pizza or something."

She breathed a sigh of relief. Spencer would be along. That would keep things safe and light, the way she wanted them to remain. Safe and at a distance. "That would be nice," she said.

It *would* be nice, he thought. Even the fact that she and Spencer would probably wear him out, it would still be fun. Just like a real family again.

Chapter Nine

"Uh-oh." Mark drove into the driveway and parked behind a gray Cadillac.

The license plate on the Cadillac read Aero One.

"Your father-in-law is here?"

"Yes."

"Is that bad?"

Mark hesitated a little too long to make his reassurance convincing. "No, it's no problem." *I hope.*

Alabama Avenue was wide and tree-lined, with live oak branches arching over the road and meeting in the center. All the lawns on Mark's block were deep with sweeping drives that led to three- and four-car garages. The houses were large and new and, Leah figured, probably very expensive.

She glanced at Mark as he turned off the engine. It didn't at all seem his type of place. She knew enough about him to know that he didn't fit into the well-manicured mold. There was something in his eyes that almost longed for open spaces and fresh breezes. It was as if he had purposefully hemmed himself into a hermetically sealed world where the air couldn't touch him.

They opened their doors and climbed from the warm car into the wintry air. Hurrying up to the door, Mark fumbled for his door key.

"You need a wreath, Mark."

"A wreath?"

"Yes, you know—a Christmas wreath. You do celebrate Christmas, don't you?"

He located the key. "Well, Santa Claus comes, if that's what you mean."

Her breath was an audible huff. "No, that's not what I mean."

Before Mark could turn the key, the door was opened by Abel Constance.

"There you are," he said, none too pleasantly. "I've been looking for you all afternoon."

Mark and Leah stepped into the foyer and shook the frigid air from their bodies. Mark helped Leah with her coat and hung it on the rack before removing his.

"Hello, Abel. Sorry, I was out of the office this afternoon."

"I noticed."

"Do you remember Leah Johnson?"

Abel's piercing eyes scanned the bulky sweater and fatigue pants she was wearing, then landed at the high-top sneakers on her feet. "Certainly," he said, lifting his eyes to her face. "The piano teacher."

Leah didn't miss his distaste for the way she was dressed, but she just smiled and said, "Hello, Mr. Constance."

"How did you know I had the piano delivered this afternoon?"

Mark and Leah glanced at each other quickly, then Mark said, "Well, I didn't."

"Really?" Abel's critical gaze ran the length of her again. "I just assumed that you had gone to pick her up for the lesson or something."

"No."

"Oh."

Tired of waiting for Mark to explain, Leah said, "We're taking Spencer to dinner."

"Dad! Leah!" Spencer bounded down the stairway. "We're gonna go to dinner? Where?"

Leah bent over and gave Spencer a hug. "Hi, kiddo. Yes, we're going to dinner. You'll have to ask your dad where."

She noticed that Mark and Spencer didn't have a hug for each other. And Mark also seemed extremely distracted with his father-in-law around. She suspected her presence had something to do with that.

"Where, Dad?"

"Some place that has pizza, I guess."

"Pizza Hut!" cried Spencer. "Let's go to Pizza Hut. Hey, come look what Grandfather Constance bought me."

"You're welcome to come with us, Abel," said Mark, knowing full well what would be the man's reaction to eating pizza for dinner.

"Thank you, but I have plans for the evening. I believe Spencer now has something to show you."

Mark cringed inwardly at the frigid tone in Abel's voice. It was the distinct sound of displeasure, but whether because Mark had disappeared all afternoon or because he was taking Leah Johnson to dinner, he didn't know.

"Look, guys," said Spencer. In one corner of the living room the furniture had been pushed aside and in its place was a black baby grand piano. Spencer sat on the bench and began banging away. "Isn't it neat!"

"Beautiful," said Leah as she walked over for a closer inspection.

"Goodness, Abel," said Mark. "You didn't have to do this."

Abel's chin jutted out. "He is my grandson. If he wants to learn music, he should have a proper instrument." He leaned close to Mark. "He should have proper instruction, also. What are her qualifications?"

"Qualifications?" How the hell was he supposed to know what her qualifications were? She taught his son to play "Jingle Bells" on an old upright crammed against a cluttered wall of her cluttered house. "Julliard," he whispered to Abel.

"Really?"

Mark pursed his lips and nodded. Then, before Abel could ask any more questions that he'd have to lie about, he ambled over to the piano to join Leah and Spencer.

"What do you think, Spence?" Mark smiled. "This is really something, isn't it?"

Spencer's eyes were lit up like Christmas lights. "I love it! Watch this." With his right hand, he began picking out the notes for "Jingle Bells," performing a tune that sounded only vaguely like the original.

Leah grinned at Mark and put her finger to her lip so he wouldn't say anything to dampen Spencer's enthusiasm.

Mark didn't notice. He was aware only of the grim line of Abel's mouth. For years, he had done nothing to cause Abel displeasure. For years, he had cultivated himself into the image his father-in-law wanted. Had he now, in one afternoon, blown ten years of that subservience and cultivation?

"Miss Johnson," said Abel. "You are going to teach him the classics, aren't you? Bach, Chopin, that sort of thing?"

Spencer was making a sour face, but Leah said, "Of course, Mr. Constance." Then she elbowed

Spencer in the side and said, "Plus a little classic rock and roll."

He brightened immediately. "Yeah!" He began banging once again on the piano, while Leah watched and laughed at his antics.

Abel took Mark by the arm and led him across the room to speak privately. "Where were you this afternoon? I needed to talk about the Five-O fighter project."

Mark suddenly felt as if he was ten years old and was being disciplined after school by the principal. He didn't owe Abel any explanations. It was his life, dammit! He was senior vice-president of the company. He didn't have to punch any time clock.

All indignation aside, he had to admit that the life he led *was* a life that Abel had created.

"Sorry, Abel. I had some things outside the office I needed to take care of."

"As with Miss Johnson, for instance?"

Mark knew Abel wasn't upset that he was taking a woman to dinner. He had often mentioned that he wanted Mark to find someone to date. When Angela ran off with another man to New Mexico, Abel abruptly relinquished all parental ties to his only daughter. She was cut off from his life. Mark had then become the replacement, the child Abel had lost. The life to dominate. And he wasn't at all opposed to Mark finding another woman. But Mark felt sure that

Abel had someone a little different from Leah John-son in mind.

"She's been helping me locate Pop." The half-truth stuck in his chest, fueling more self-disgust.

"And have you found him?"

"Yes."

"Where is he?"

Mark's past was so foreign to Abel, it had always made Mark uncomfortable and embarrassed to bring it up. Although Abel liked to make a big deal of it in public, telling everyone how he had created a new Mark Carruthers, referring to himself as Pygmalion and to Mark as his creation brought to life, Mark still had trouble talking about it. He had put up with Abel's favorite tale for so long now, it was too late to start complaining. Still, it always embarrassed him to make any reference to his past at all.

"He is visiting a relative," he mumbled. "Up on the mountain."

Abel shook his head. "Some people just never change."

"Thank heaven for that," said Leah, walking up to the two men. She had obviously overheard and was now staring pointedly at Mark, as if she expected him to say something. He didn't have the faintest idea what he was supposed to say. She probably wanted him to defend Pop or something, he figured.

Abel caught the silent exchange between the two of them and was confused. "How did you happen to know where he had gone?"

"Leah found out and told me."

"How did you find out, Miss Johnson?"

"Mr. Carruthers came into the DeHaven Center to buy something. I wasn't there when he was, but when I came to work yesterday around noon, the owner told me he had come in and where he had gone."

"You work at the DeHaven Center?" Abel asked above the din Spencer was creating at the piano.

"Yes."

His gaze jumped from Leah to Mark then back to her again. "I thought you taught music?"

"Oh, I do. I'm the music director at the Eastside Congregational Church, and I teach private piano lessons, but I also work at the DeHaven Center."

"Why?"

Taken aback by the way he asked, she glanced at Mark. He was no help at all. He looked as if he had just swallowed a whole turnip.

"I like working there, Mr. Constance."

"I see."

Mark couldn't take any more of this. "I'm going to go change for dinner." He walked away, leaving Abel and Leah scowling at his back.

"Something is definitely wrong with him today," Abel mused aloud.

What was wrong, Leah knew, was his dependence on and fear of his father-in-law. But she wasn't about to say that. "Probably he's just worried about his father."

Abel laughed. "I don't think you understand the relationship between Mark and his father very well, Miss Johnson. Mark has been wanting him out of the house for a long time. The man is an incredible burden."

Leah's mouth tightened into a straight thin line. "He is a wonderful old man. Kind and fun-loving."

Abel looked surprised. "You've met him?"

She kept her voice under the strictest control. "Spencer and I drove up into the mountains to see him yesterday."

"You—you took Spencer up into the hills! To one of those relative's shacks!"

"Yes."

"Mark approved of that?"

"Mr. Constance, Pop is Spencer's grandfather. Just as you are. He wanted to see him."

A flow of ice crept down from the Arctic and slid like a glacier over his face. "The man is nothing like I am," he said slowly and precisely. "He is crude, annoying, ignorant."

The momentary stunned silence in the living room became like a roar in Leah's ears. She realized that Spencer had stopped playing the piano and was staring at the two of them.

Suddenly, he banged his hands against the piano keys and stood up, his small face red and drawn tight. "He is not ignorant!" he yelled at Abel. He came over to stand in front of them with his fists balled tight at his side. "He's the best grandpa in the whole world! You're the worst!"

"Go to your room," said his grandfather.

Spencer stuck out his chin. "I won't. You can't make me!"

Leah felt as if she'd been hit by a truck. "Spencer!" she cried. "Don't talk to your grandfather that way."

"I will if I want to!"

"What's going on here?" Mark came down the stairs in record time. "What's all this yelling?"

Leah hung back, numbed by the anger and the bitterness. Abel's face was red, and he was stammering as if he had never been talked back to in his life.

In horror, Leah watched him raise his arm to strike the boy. Before she could reach out to stop him, Mark's hand grasped the older man's wrist. It was held, suspended in the air, while the two men glared at each other. "No, Abel," he said sharply.

The older man looked at him in surprise. Mark had never defied him before. Abel couldn't believe he was doing it now.

Mark brought the man's arm down to his side, but he hesitated before releasing it. "I don't know what Spencer did. But I won't allow you to hit him."

Abel's blustering had turned to mute shock. Without a glance at Spencer or at Mark, he picked up his coat from a nearby chair and slipped it on. He walked to the door, opened it, then looked back. "I expect an explanation for what is going on here, Mark," he said. He looked at Leah. "Ever since you came along...I don't know—things are changed." Then he stepped out and closed the door behind him.

The three of them stood staring at the closed door. Finally, Mark broke the strained silence. "What in hell happened down here?"

The pain and empathy Leah felt for Spencer became anger against the boy's father. "Why don't you ask your son?"

Mark absorbed the cold tone in her voice. "Okay." He looked at Spencer. "What happened?"

Spencer's face was pinched, and he looked as if he was about to cry. His fists were clenched in tight balls, and his arms hung rigid at his side. "I hate him."

Mark said nothing for a long moment. Leah, still numb, watched from the sidelines. Finally Mark spoke. "You said that to him?"

It took Spencer a bit to answer. "I told him he was the worst grandpa."

Mark's breath came out in a loud whoosh.

"He said mean things about Pop," said Spencer. "He said he was ignorant and a bunch of other stuff, too."

Mark didn't know what to say or do. Everything, it seemed, was falling apart. He had worked all his life to get where he was. And he had given credit for most of what he had to Abel, the man who had nurtured him through the early years, introduced him to all the right people, believed in his designs, taught him how to be the person he wanted to be.

"This is how I repay him," he mumbled aloud to himself.

Leah's gaze narrowed on his face. "Repay who?"

He looked up, surprised to have spoken aloud. "Abel."

"I don't believe you," she said with a shake of her head. "He says horrible things about your father and you're worried about Abel's feelings? I mean, I don't care if you defend what I do in front of your father-in-law. That doesn't really matter. But to not defend your own father..."

"You don't understand."

"I do!" yelled Spencer as he ran toward the stairs. He climbed halfway up, then looked down. "You hate Pop just because he doesn't have money like Grandfather Constance. You hate him because you were poor!" Before Mark could react, Spencer dashed up the remaining stairs and ran down the hallway to his bedroom. The door slammed shut, and the finality of the sound echoed through the stark, cavernous house.

Leah's attention was fixed on Mark. He, too, appeared as if he were about to crumble. She wanted to hate him. She wanted to equate him with her own uncaring father, to blame him for all the hurt she had known. She wanted to lash out and yell at him the way Spencer had, but when his eyes landed on her, and she saw the deep, raw hurt mirrored there, she knew she could not hate him. She knew she felt something she had never before felt for anyone.

She stepped up to him and rested her cool palm against his hot cheek. His eyes closed briefly, then settled on her face. "What's happening to my life?" he questioned aloud. "Everything was so...so perfect for a while."

"Fantasies usually are."

His eyebrows drew together. "What do you mean?"

He didn't get it. He didn't see that all he had created was an illusion. He was not the Mark Carruthers that Abel Constance wanted him to be. Why couldn't he admit that? It was so evident in his eyes and in his voice. He wanted his son to love him. He had been worried to death when his father was missing. He was a man who cared deeply about those around him, but for some reason, he just couldn't admit it.

She let her hand drop and shook her head. "Have I told you you're a mess, Carruthers?"

"I believe you have."

After a moment, she said, "Maybe you should go talk to your son."

Mark's gaze traveled up the staircase. It was obvious he was scared to death. "I don't even know what to say to him anymore, Leah."

"How about, I love you."

He glanced back at her, wishing for the feel of her soft hand against his face. Wishing he could wrap her around him like a warm, woolen blanket. If he did, he would never let her go. "I do, you know."

"I know that. But maybe you should tell him."

He plunged his hands into the pockets of his suit trousers. "I think he blames me for running off his mother."

"Maybe he just wants to know he hasn't been completely abandoned."

His eyes traveled slowly over her face, drinking in the beauty and comfort she so easily gave to others. "You know, it scares me—the thought of being both mother and father to him."

"Don't try to be, Mark. Just be the best father you can be. Be the kind of father Pop was to you."

Mark glanced at her sharply, completely caught off guard. "What—"

"He was, wasn't he, Mark?"

Mark couldn't answer.

"He didn't have money to give you the education you wanted or the clothes you wanted or all the things that rich city kids had, but he was a good father, wasn't he?''

Mark's eyes closed as memories came back, memories he had shut out for too many years. There were those of his dad taking him hunting for the first time. There were the times, working side by side in the tool shed while a heavy rain hammered down on the corrugated tin roof. There were nights, sitting on the porch together, just listening to the sound of crickets' wings filling up the darkness.

"He was a good father," he said quietly. "Probably the best."

"Did you ever tell him that?"

Mark shook his head.

She almost cried. She had to fight to hold back the tears. Too many painful memories of her own crowded into her mind. Too many times when she wanted her father to love her, to pay attention to her. Too many times when she had wished for a real family, one that would always be there for her, one that wouldn't shut her out.

"Go talk to Spencer, Mark."

Looking at her, he saw the wetness in her eyes. But right now, he couldn't even ask her about it. His mind was centered on Spencer and on Pop and on all the things he wished he had said and done. Leah was right. Now was his chance to say some of them.

Before he chickened out, he went to the stairs and began to climb. It was a slow climb, endlessly long, with fear and the possibility of rejection waiting at the end of the line.

As she watched his reluctant climb, Leah came to a startling revelation. She never wanted to get involved with Mark. She only wanted to be friends with Spencer and to help the two of them learn to love each other. She didn't want to be a part of that love. The thought of it scared her to death. Once Mark no longer needed her help, he might no longer need her.

Unlike all the others before him, he had promised her nothing. Still, what he had given her in the short time they had known each other would hurt badly when it was taken away.

She didn't want to, but she did. She loved Mark Carruthers.

Chapter Ten

Mark lifted his hand to knock, but paused. He had known a lot of rejection in his life, but none of it came close to comparing with the rejection of a son for his father. He had done that to Pop, he realized now. He had rejected him as a father. And now, it was very possible that Spencer would do the same thing to him.

He knocked lightly. There was no answer. He tried again and said, "Spence?"

"What?" came the muffled answer.

"May I come in?"

"What for?"

"I want to talk to you."

"What for?"

Mark tried the doorknob. It wasn't locked. He opened it slowly, and his eyes scanned the large, messy bedroom until they landed on Spencer, scrunched down low in the corner, almost swallowed up by a big red beanbag chair. He was scowling at the intruder standing in his doorway.

"I just want to talk to you, Spencer."

When there was no reply, Mark stepped in and closed the door behind him. He walked to the corner and scooted a blue beanbag chair next to the red one. He eased himself into the cushion and smiled. "It may take a crane to get me out of here."

His son didn't crack a smile.

Mark didn't know where to begin, so he just said, "I think there are some things that need to be straightened out between us. Don't you?"

Spencer shrugged and picked up his Rubik's Cube. He had solved it when he was seven, but he still liked to play around with it sometimes. Now seemed like a good time.

"I've made some mistakes," said Mark. "Probably even more than I realize. I mean, you've probably got a list a mile long of all the things I've done wrong, don't you?"

Spencer concentrated on the cube. "Not really."

"Oh, come on, now," urged his father. "I know you're mad at me and upset with me over lots of things. I—I just want you to tell me what they are, so we can talk about them."

He watched while Spencer cranked and turned the cube and got all the yellow squares on one side. Finally, the boy said, "Okay. How come you work all the time?"

Mark heaved a sigh of relief. At least they were starting with the easy questions. This one he could answer. "I work so we'll have money. So I can buy nice things for you—and for me. Things I never had when I was growing up."

"What if I don't want all this junk?"

Mark's gaze circled the room, a room that was brimming over with Nintendo games and a computer, a television, radio, bunk beds, Lego, G.I. Joe figures and planes and headquarters, books, tapes, chemistry sets, a microscope, stuffed animals, plastic models. The room was FAO Schwartz and NASA all rolled into one.

"You've never been without all these toys and gadgets, Spencer. You have no idea what it's like."

"You got to play outside all the time when you were a kid," the boy grumbled. "You got to fish and shoot guns and all sorts of neat stuff."

"There was nothing else to do," said Mark, marveling at the fact that such a humdrum childhood sounded exciting to Spencer. Growing up, he would have given his eyeteeth to have even a quarter of the things his son had. He had never looked at all those things he did as a kid as fun.

"You've never taken me fishin'," the boy complained. "Pop's taken me, but you never have."

"I didn't realize it was something you wanted to do so badly. I'll take you fishing sometime, Spence."

The boy looked at him for the first time, but his glance was cautious and his voice tentative. "You will?"

"Sure."

"When?"

"I don't know, I—" He saw that Spencer's eyes had glazed over once again and he'd turned back to the toy in his hand. "Okay," he thought aloud, realizing that some sort of commitment was needed here. "Uh, how about next week?"

Spencer dropped the cube. "Really? You promise?"

Mark wasn't used to making promises to his son. Only to his boss, to his father-in-law. But maybe it was time to start changing that. "I promise. Of course, we'll have to find a stream that isn't frozen over."

"We could go up to Cus'n Cooter's and fish there. It wasn't frozen."

"Well," hedged Mark, uncomfortable with the thought, "we'll, uh, we'll see about that."

Silence fell over the room. It would have been easy to take the small victory and leave it at that, but Mark knew there was much more than the need for a fishing trip between them. He could see other questions hovering around Spencer's mouth and lingering in his eyes.

"Daddy?" he finally asked. "Why don't you like Pop?"

A fistlike pain hit Mark in the midsection. "I like Pop, son."

Spencer shook his head. "You wanted him to go away. You're always upset with him. Every time he's around, you're always mad."

"That's not true," said Mark, as the blood began to pound in his temples.

"It is true. You're always so nice to Grandfather Constance. You do stuff with him all the time. You're different with him than with Pop."

"You don't understand. There's a difference."

"Yeah," said Spencer. "And I know what that difference is. Grandfather Constance is an old moneybags and Pop is poor."

"That's no way to talk about your grandfather."

"Which one?" he spat.

Mark took a deep breath to collect his thoughts. This conversation could easily get out of hand. His head was throbbing just from the thought of it. "Look," he said with as much calm as he could muster. "My relationship with my father is—well, it's sometimes difficult, that's all." He reached over and laid his hand on Spencer's knee. "But I promise you this, Spence. I'll try harder, okay? I'll try not to get mad at Pop."

"It's too late."

"Why do you say that?"

"Because he's gone."

"He'll come back, son. He's just visiting Cooter for a few days. Believe me, Pop will be back before the week is out."

Spencer knew he wouldn't, but he didn't say that. Instead, he said, "Daddy, where are all the photo albums?"

Mark frowned. "Which ones?"

"All of them. The ones of me as a baby. And the ones of you—and Mommy."

The pain in Mark's stomach moved to his chest. "Well, they're, uh, put up somewhere. In the attic. What do you want them for?"

"Just to look at."

The guilt was what he couldn't live with. For two years now, Mark had been able to handle the arguments, the silences, the irritation, the loneliness. But what he couldn't handle was the guilt. A mother had left her young child, and somehow Mark knew he was to blame. Something had gone unsaid or undone. He hadn't changed enough to suit her. He hadn't been the husband he should have been. He hadn't been able to keep her. And what was worse, he had not even cared if she stayed or not. If he had—if he had cared enough—his son would have a mother.

"I'll dig them out, okay?" he said gently, his hand moving to his son's arm.

Spencer picked up the Rubik's Cube and tossed it between his hands. "I sometimes forget what she looked like."

"Me, too."

Spencer glanced up, surprised. "You forgot, too?"

"I have lots of pictures of her in my head. Sometimes they get all mixed up."

"She didn't love us, did she, Dad?"

He hesitated, wanting to answer truthfully but painlessly. "Not the way we wanted her to, I guess."

In one hurtling motion, Spencer threw himself toward his father and wrapped his arms around his neck. His small face was buried against Mark's throat. "I love you, Daddy."

Mark squeezed his eyes shut and held his son tight. He had come up here to tell Spencer he loved him. He had wanted so badly to say the words, but he had been afraid. Now, his son had had the courage to say them first.

"I love you, too," he whispered against his son's hair, knowing how much he meant it, only wishing he'd had the guts to say it first.

"I'M STUFFED," said Mark, leaning back into Leah's couch. He stretched his legs out in front of him and folded his hands behind his head. "How about you two?"

Leah was sitting on the floor in front of her Christmas tree, still working on her last piece of pizza. "Almost stuffed."

Spencer had taken all the pepperoni and sausage off his piece, and now he was popping them in one at a time. "Not me. I want dessert."

"Ugh," groaned Mark, but he only half meant it. He was feeling great. Better than he had felt in a long, long time. It was a meal with no pretensions, no dos and don'ts, no rights or wrongs. He didn't have to watch everything he said and did around Leah. He didn't have to pretend. She looked beautiful to him, sitting there before a backdrop of colorful lights, munching on a big slice of pizza.

Christmas music played on the stereo, and the two cats were curled up under the tree.

"I'm glad we decided to get the pizza to go."

"Me, too," said Mark, and he meant it. There was still something about her house that made him feel a bit off balance, but it was nothing like that first evening he had come here to collect Spencer. It didn't bother him so much because he realized it fit her. An energetic mass of colorful chaos. That's what Leah was. And that was what her house reflected.

"We used to have one of those little things," he said, pointing to the angel chime on top of the piano.

"Isn't that pretty? I got that at the center."

"Yeah," he mumbled, looking away. "I'm sure that's where we got ours, too."

Leah studied Mark's angular profile. He was all hard bones and angles, full of masculine defiance and challenge. And yet, underneath, he was soft and emotional and oh, so vulnerable. "My mother had one," she said softly. "It was very expensive. Came from Germany, I believe." She looked over at the chime on her piano. "It wasn't half as pretty as this one."

"Were you rich?" asked Spencer, his mouth full of food.

Leah was aware that Mark was watching her. She could feel the heat from his eyes landing against her cheek. "My parents had lots of money," she answered.

"So you were rich, then," said Spencer logically.

She glanced at Mark for only a fraction of a second then centered her gaze on the boy. "There are all kinds of riches, Spencer. My family was rich with money but we were very poor in other ways."

"Yeah? Like how?"

"We weren't a family. We weren't close. We never talked much to each other. We went our separate ways."

"How is that poor?"

Her eyes caught the flickering lights on the tree and she focused on it. Mark's own gaze narrowed slightly as he watched her. He had never bothered to ask her about her family. He had never wanted to hear that she'd had more money than he'd had. He wondered why she had turned away from her family's wealth. If her parents were rich, she could have had anything she wanted, and yet she had chosen to live in the inner city and to devote her life to charity work. Why did she do it? And why did she look so sad?

It struck him, for the first time, that maybe Leah Johnson was lonely. She was so full of life, it was difficult to conceive of her having a void in her life. But he saw that she did. She had wanted a family. It was reflected in the depths of her eyes.

"I feel richer right now," she said, still focusing on the tree lights, "sitting here with you and your father, than I've ever felt in my life."

Spencer screwed up his nose, shrugged and went back to his pizza.

But Mark got it. And what else he got was the shocking realization that he had fallen in love. Not just the kind of love that would move him up the corporate or social ladder. But another kind. The kind that felt warm and secure and as inevitable as the rise and fall of the sun and moon.

It was a realization that scared him. He didn't know how on earth that kind of love and this woman were supposed to fit into his life.

"Can we spend Christmas here?"

It took Mark a minute to focus on Spencer's question. "Why?"

"'Cause she has a tree."

"We have a tree."

Spencer made a face. "Dad thinks that big moldy thing in our living room is a Christmas tree."

"The Leicester sculpture," Mark said. "What, you don't like it, either?"

Leah drew her knees up and wrapped her arms around her legs. "That's a Christmas tree? I was trying this afternoon to figure out what it was."

"I want a real tree," said Spencer.

"Everyone should have a real one," agreed Leah.

Mark didn't agree. "You forget to water them, and they lose all their needles in the carpet. They're a mess."

"You're a grinch."

Spencer laughed, and Mark looked affronted. Leah was sitting on the floor in front of him, so he picked up one leg and wrapped it around one side of her, while his other leg captured her from the other side. He leaned forward and encircled her neck with his arms, completely capturing her.

"What did you call me?" he growled against her neck.

Leah laughed. "That tickles."

"She called you a grinch, Dad. Are you gonna beat her up?"

Mark grasped her under the arms and pulled her up over his lap and onto the couch. "I've got a better idea. Ticklish, are you?"

"No, Mark, don't you dare. I mean it!"

His assault was merciless. And to top it off, Spencer piled on top and began an assault of his own.

When Leah's breathless pleas finally persuaded them to stop, they all lay in an exhausted, laughing pile, half on the couch and half off.

Spencer jumped up to flip the tape over on the stereo, and Leah was left with Mark sprawled over her. He was smiling at her and, with his face free of tension for the first time, he looked years younger. He kissed her lightly on the lips, and she felt the strain in both their bodies, the need for more than playful kisses. A need that both knew would have to wait.

He helped her to sit up on the couch. Spencer came over and sat on the floor in front of them.

"What are we going to do tomorrow?"

Mark and Leah looked at each other.

"I've got to work," said Mark.

"I have lessons all morning," Leah said. "And I promised Lilla that I'd run the center for her tomorrow afternoon. She has a doctor's appointment."

"Oh," said Spencer, reaching for his can of Coke on the coffee table.

The moment of merriment was lost, but the physical tension between Mark and Leah seemed to grow stronger by the minute.

Mark knew they should pack up and go home, but he couldn't make himself say the words. He needed so badly to touch her. He wanted just a few minutes with her alone.

She knew she ought to stand up and clean up the mess left from the pizza. But she was afraid if she did, they would go. She didn't want them to leave. She felt restless with the needs he stirred in her. She longed for a moment alone with him.

"So I have to stay with Clara again tomorrow?" Spencer asked dejectedly.

Mark's brain had come unfused. He had trouble connecting the different parts. Spencer's questions. His own needs. Leah's soft skin. The loneliness of a child. The needs of a woman. The complexities of this relationship.

"I—I suppose so," he finally said to the boy.

Leah, too, searched for order in the chaos that existed in her mind. Too many years of hurt and loneliness had made her fearful of what she was feeling. Her heart was at stake. Her emotional sanity.

She glanced at Spencer, realizing that he, too, had needs. "You could work with me at the center, Spencer. I mean—that is, if it's all right with your father."

"Can I, Dad?" he asked eagerly. "Can I?"

Mark's eyes focused on the coffee table rather than on them. The DeHaven Center. His son, working there. "Well," he said, hesitating.

"Please, Daddy."

It implied so much. He just wasn't sure.

He looked at Spencer and wondered, would it hurt? But it did hurt. It hurt from his head to his toes. Still, he knew he couldn't say no. "I guess it would be all right." He glanced at Leah uneasily. Would it be all right, or was it laying a trap for his son, a trap like the one he had been in for so many years?

Looking at her was his downfall. The soft eagerness in her warm eyes made him realize that everything was all right with the world. There were no differences in class. There was no good or bad. There was only now, with the three of them together.

Tomorrow, he knew, it would all look different. But, for now, it was good and right and very real.

"Sure, Spencer," he said, warmed by the spontaneous hug his son gave him.

"Why don't you let him spend the night?" she suggested. "That way he'll be here in the morning when I have to go in to work. I have a sleeping bag around here somewhere."

"Yes!" cried Spencer. "A sleepover. Daddy can stay, too."

Leah and Mark exchanged another strained look between them. Tension was growing by the minute.

"I don't think so, Spence," said Mark. "But you can stay."

"Where's the sleeping bag, Leah?"

"Well, let's go look for it."

Mark stayed on the couch and watched them. Leah opened the hall closet and the contents almost came tumbling out. It was unbelievable. Not one of his closets looked like that. They were neat and orderly, everything in its place. The antithesis of the way he had grown up, with debris strewn everywhere around him. His mother had tried to keep things neat and tidy, but there hadn't really been anywhere to keep stuff. And the yard was always filled with rusted junk that Pop was someday going to work on. Along with the memories, Mark had removed all clutter from his life.

Leah obviously had no such need.

He turned his eyes on the tree. "Love Came Down at Christmas" played softly on the tape deck. He squinted his eyes, and the lights and the colorful balls danced. For the briefest of moments, he once again felt young and hopeful, all of life stretched out like an endless smorgasbord in front of him.

He stopped squinting, and the real world came back in focus. At least the world he had convinced himself was real. Leah had called his life a fantasy. Was that what it had been? Had he been fooling himself all these years?

Spencer and Leah came into the room with a sleeping bag.

"You ready to hit the sack, Spence?" Mark asked hopefully.

"No. I want dessert."

"Dessert. Oh."

Leah led the boy around the counter into the small kitchen. "I've got just the thing for you here. Fudge." She uncovered the pan and sliced several squares, setting them on a plate. "You want some, Mark?"

Fantasy, reality. Looking at this beautiful, giving woman who could offer his son so much, he wondered which it was he was seeing. The reality of what his life could become. Or just another fantasy, and one that would not mesh with the one he already lived.

Leah walked over and stood in front of him, looking down. Smiling. He reached up and took a piece from the plate of fudge she was offering. And he knew that, whatever she offered him, he would reach for it like a starving animal, one that had been left outside in the cold for too long.

SPENCER HAD FALLEN ASLEEP on the couch, and Mark carried him into the room where Leah had laid out the sleeping bag. He tucked him in and brushed back a lock of pale hair that fell across his face.

"He looks peaceful, doesn't he?" Mark whispered, squatting down to cover the sleeping boy.

"He looks loved."

Mark looked up at Leah, but her face stayed in a shadow he could not read.

He stood up, and together they left the room.

"Well," she said, when they stood alone in the living room. Now that Spencer was asleep, the buffer was gone. She wasn't sure she was ready to face Mark or her convoluted feelings.

"Why did you look as if you were going to cry?"

She spun around, startled. "What do you mean?"

"At my house this evening. When you—it was when you convinced me that I needed to go up and talk to Spencer."

She turned away. "I don't remember."

"Don't remember or don't want to tell me?"

"Would you like some tea?"

He came up behind her and gently turned her around. "Yes, and don't change the subject."

She searched the floor between them for an answer. "I guess I just felt badly for you and Spencer."

"It was more than that, Leah."

She stepped around the counter and picked up the teapot. She turned on the faucet and filled it. "I just didn't have the best of relationships with my parents, that's all. I guess I was remembering things—the not so good times."

Standing in the living room, he rested his forearms on the counter. "What were they like?"

"My parents?"

"Yes."

"Oh, vague. About me, that is. Busy. Much too busy for a child."

"The money—the fact that you were rich, that didn't mean anything to you, did it?"

"It meant I was sent to private schools. It meant summer camps and separate vacations. It meant searching for a replacement."

He frowned as he watched her put the teapot on the burner. "What do you mean?"

"Nothing. Forget it."

"No, I really want to know. Replacement for what? For your parents?"

She grabbed two cups from the dish rack and set them on the counter. She took a deep breath and looked directly at him. "For love, Mark. I spent my life looking for love."

"With other men, you mean."

"Surprised? Are you shocked to know that Miss Goody Two Shoes Johnson has been around the block a time or two?"

"I wasn't thinking that. Is that the way you see it?"

She shook her head, opened a canister and pulled out two tea bags.

When she didn't answer, he said, "Maybe it's easier for you to look at it that way, as some sort of tawdry period of your life."

She planted a hand at her waist. "Instead of what?" she snapped.

"Instead of facing the fact that you got hurt."

"What makes you think I got hurt?"

He shrugged. "Well, you're not married. You're not even dating, as far as I can see. You live alone. You devote all your time to making the world a peachy place to live. You live like some sort of nun, working over everybody else's lives so you don't have to do anything about your own."

The teapot began to whistle, but Leah didn't move to retrieve it. She was staring at Mark, stunned by the accusations.

"That's not true."

Mark came around the counter and took the teapot off the stove. He set it down on the tile counter and stood in front of Leah. "It is true. And I don't think I really realized it until tonight. I've been so busy worrying about my own problems. But it struck me—remember when you said that you felt richer sitting here with Spence and me?"

She wouldn't answer. She wouldn't even look at him.

He cupped her chin in his hand and tilted her face. "Remember, Leah?"

"I remember," she said quietly, her mouth thin and tight.

His eyes fixed on her mouth, then he ran the tip of his finger over her lips, softening them. "That's when it hit me. I sort of knew in that moment that you've been treated badly in love."

"That's not the only reason I do what I do. I enjoy helping people."

"I know that. And you're very... I don't know—giving. I don't think I've ever known anyone who gives as much as you do."

His fingers traced the outline of her jaw, his thumb stroking over her mouth once more.

"You should take a little for yourself, Leah."

Her eyes closed as the sensation of those fingers took control of her reason. "I've heard it all before."

His other hand came up to the side of her head, and his fingers combed through her hair. "Empty promises, you mean?"

Her eyes remained closed, and she rested the weight of her head against his hand. "Every one in the book."

He knew he should stop before things got out of hand. He knew it was all wrong. How could he promise her things then let her go? Was he going to do the same thing to her that every other man had done? He didn't want to. God, he didn't want to. But he didn't know where his own life was going. He felt as if he were falling, tumbling backward and forward from one life to another. He didn't know where the reality lay anymore. He was already lost, but he shouldn't drag Leah with him.

"I won't treat you badly," he heard himself say, and his mouth came down to meet hers. She tasted warm and soft and pliable in his arms.

Leah parted her lips for him. He held her secure and solid, and she wanted to stay this way forever.

His hand moved from the side of her face, down her neck and onto the front of her sweater. The heat from his fingers melted into her flesh, and she pressed into him, wanting to absorb the pressure of his hands.

Promises, she told herself. *He has promised you nothing. Only his hands, and his mouth, and the long hard length of his body.* That was the only promise she wanted right now. It was the one she craved.

He pressed her against the counter, and the hard edge dug into her back. His hand came around her hips to cushion her from his weight. His mouth had become a part of her, his tongue plunging into the deep recesses of her mouth. When it moved away to her jaw and down to her neck, she felt a sense of loss.

His hand slipped beneath her sweater and glided over her bare skin.

"You feel so good," he breathed against her throat. "So soft." And although the need in him was like a fire-breathing dragon, his mind retained the picture of his sleeping child in the next room. He knew he would have to content himself with the taste of her mouth and the subtlest touches of her body.

Leah, too, was aware of the presence in her house, a presence that could guide her to sanity, that could give her time to think about what she was doing with this man. His hands swept all sense of reason away. His mouth took her into a world all its own.

She tried to find her breath. "Mark," she sighed against his chest. "This is happening so fast."

"You want it slow," he whispered against her ear, "I can go slow."

"Please, Mark."

His hand held her hips in place against him, but the fingers that stroked her breast slipped slowly down to her waist and out from under her sweater. He grasped the back of her head and laid his forehead against hers.

Her hands were looped around his neck, and she slowly slid them around to the front until her palms lay flat against his chest. It rose and fell with quick, uneven breaths. She took a deep one to still the racing of her heart. "He's at a very impressionable age, you know."

The hand that pressed against her hips rose to her waist. His eyes closed as he tried to focus on the reality of the moment. "So am I," he said with a ragged sigh.

She giggled softly and wriggled from his embrace. She laid her hand against the side of the teapot. "The water's cold."

"I don't want tea," he said, watching her.

She took another deep breath. "You have to work tomorrow."

He leaned against the counter and, with his hand, massaged the back of his neck. "Yeah. Unfortunately."

"I'm glad you're letting Spencer stay with me tomorrow, Mark."

His eyes moved up her body and over her face. He had to get out of here. Fast. He couldn't keep looking at her and not touch her. Child or no child, he was tempted to make love to her under the Christmas tree and on the kitchen counter and behind the couch. God, he had to get out of here. "Yeah, me, too," he mumbled, heading for the living room. He grabbed his coat and slipped it on in record time.

The eagerness they had both shown toward each other was now directed at getting him out of the house as fast as possible. They both knew it was the only way. The lingering taste and feel of each other was too strong and too binding to deny much longer.

"I'll pick up Spencer tomorrow after work."

"Shall I fix you some dinner then?"

His sigh, this time, was one of disgust. "No, Abel and I are entertaining some clients." Despite the risk, his gaze swept over her. "I wish I could get out of it."

"When are you going to go talk to Pop?"

He opened the front door and let the cold winter wind do to his body what his own mind could not. "I don't know."

"Are you afraid to go get him, Mark? To go up there on the mountain?"

He stepped onto the front stoop. The dark night hid his lie. "Of course not. I'll do it, Leah. Maybe Saturday. Will—will you go with me?"

"Of course I will."

Of course she would, he thought, looking at her standing in the warm light of her doorway. Whatever he asked, he knew Leah Johnson would give. But what, he wondered painfully, could he give her in return?

Before he reached for the warmth and security of her arms, he fled down the sidewalk and into his car. He drove home to his big expensive house. His big, lonely, expensive house.

Chapter Eleven

It was a cold day, but the sun shone brightly, glinting off ice-sheathed branches of bare trees and sparkling on the tips of crackling winter grasses. The drive up the mountain had been easier than on the day Leah and Spencer had gone together. This time, they were expected. There was no icy drizzle. And Mark knew exactly which way to go.

The farther up into the mountains they drove, the quieter Mark had become. Glancing at his profile, Leah saw a muscle working nervously in his jaw. His reflective sunglasses hid the rest of his thoughts. Spencer was lying down on the back seat asleep, a *Mad* magazine covering his face. Leah tried to concentrate on the scenery around her, and the only sound around them was of spinning tires on cold wet blacktop.

Mark tried to concentrate on his driving, but so many sensations kept crowding his brain. They had become so mixed up inside him, he felt as if his muscles and tendons were tied in a hundred knots.

What was he doing here? Why had he come back? A tar-paper shack sat crooked just off the winding road, and a fat woman sat on her front porch drinking a beer. A pile of cans had been tossed into the middle of the front yard.

This was the place he had turned away from. These were the people he had left behind. *Okay, it's only temporary,* he told himself. He was just coming to see Pop, to convince him to come home again. He was simply bringing Spencer to see the relatives and to cut a Christmas tree. What was so frightening about that? Nothing, he told himself, even as the fear jumped like a nervous frog inside his stomach.

Adding to the confusion in his mind, there was Leah, smelling so sweet and looking so pretty on the seat beside him, making him want her and at the same time making him want to run as fast as he could away from her. Her hair was tied back in a ponytail, but the shorter, curly hair at the front had come loose and was falling around her face. She was wearing jeans and a cable-knit sweater, and her bulky coat and his jacket lay on the seat between them like a barricade.

He knew that she cared for him and that she had wanted him to keep touching her and kissing her the other night. But something more than Spencer in the other room had held her back. The loneliness inside her was different from his own. It was combined with lots of past hurt and future fears.

He glanced at her and caught her eye. He smiled, hoping she wasn't as afraid of him as he was of her. Her return smile was tentative.

"This is beautiful country," she said.

His gaze moved through the window beside her head and out the front windshield and to his left. He pulled the car over to the side of the road and slipped it into park. He rested his arms on the steering wheel and stared straight ahead. Opening the door, he grabbed his jacket and climbed out. He stood at the edge of the deserted road. The sun sparkled through the bank of trees beside him, and he heard the faint sounds of a thin creek trickling nearby.

Leah stared through the window at his back. He took a deep breath, and his shoulders lifted then settled back into place. His hands were pushed deeply into the pockets of his jacket, and his stance was wide. She felt drawn by the physical presence of him. The way he looked right now, solid and square and quietly observing of the world around him, was the way she would always think of him, remember him.

Mark heard the car door shut behind him, then Leah, wrapped in her woolen pea coat, was standing beside him, her fingers lightly touching his arm. "Is everything okay?" she asked softly.

He stared at her fingers on his arm then slowly he pulled his hand from his pocket and laid it across hers. He wrapped his fingers around hers and warmed them inside his grasp. "You probably think this is really stupid, don't you?"

"What's that?"

"This—" He breathed a cloud of vapor into the air and remained barricaded behind the glasses. "I don't know, this attitude of mine, this weirdness I have about being here . . . on the mountain."

"I don't think it's stupid."

He smiled at her. "Just weird, right?"

She smiled back. "Well . . . I don't really understand it. It's so beautiful here, and—and this is where you grew up." She looked at her hand in his then at his face, wishing she could see his eyes. "I like to think of you here—as a boy. I like to picture how you looked and what you might be doing."

His breath changed as he looked at her. And the grip of his fingers tightened on hers. His other hand came from his pocket and reached for the back of her neck, pulling her against his slick leather jacket. His mouth angled toward hers, his hand grasping the back of her head so she could not escape him. "I wish," he said in a low voice, "that you had been here then. I know exactly what I would have been doing." His mouth closed over hers, and she felt the contrast of the cold air circling around them with the rush of warm air that flowed between their lips.

Her fingers slid up the leather-covered arms of his jacket, and she felt his hand work its way inside her coat. "If you had been here," he breathed against her temple, "I never would have left. Ever."

She pressed her lips into his throat and tried to still the racing of her heart. "Do you realize," she said breathlessly, "where we are standing?"

With one hand still against her waist inside her coat and the other against the side of her neck, he lifted his head and looked around. He shook his head and chuckled disparagingly. He closed his eyes behind the glasses and let out another tortured sigh. "This doesn't seem to be your standard courtship, does it?"

She reached up and slipped the glasses from his face. "Is that what this is, Mark? A courtship?"

He pulled back and looked into her eyes. "I've never felt this way, Leah. God, I for sure never felt like this with Angela."

She wasn't sure she wanted to hear this from him. It sounded too good, too sure, too permanent. Each word was like a caress against her face.

"It's like there's this wildness inside me," he said quietly, his hand working its way up to the side of her breast. "I feel like a boy again, like—" He pulled back again and gazed down at her. "This is what's strange—I feel like I've never left this place when I'm with you. When I'm touching you." He frowned at her, confused. "I don't know whether that's good or bad, Leah."

She pulled her coat around her, and his hand fell away. She watched him silently.

"I know that sounds crazy," he said. "But it's the way I feel. It's like everything I've tried to leave behind is now rushing in on me, surrounding me. You feel so good to me, Leah. Right here, in this spot."

"And that worries you?"

"Yes," he said. "It worries me a lot, because it goes against everything I thought I wanted. It doesn't fit into the plan I had drawn for myself. What I have become, what Angela wanted, what Abel wanted..." He waved his arm around. "It's certainly not this."

"And what if your plan was wrong?"

"Then I've wasted a lot of years."

An uneasy silence hung between them until Leah said, "Maybe we should move on, Mark." She glanced at her watch. "It's close to noon."

"Yeah," he said. "I suppose so." He looked at the car. "I guess Spencer slept through the rest stop."

Leah reddened. "I certainly hope so."

"He really likes you, you know."

She stared at the car. "I know. He—he's very special to me, too." It was too much to think about right now. Spencer, they both knew, added a whole different dimension to their relationship. He signified a permanence that neither of them was ready to face or accept.

"Shall we forge on, then?" he asked quietly.

Leah walked to her side of the car. "Yes."

"DON'T GO RIGHT HERE," Leah warned when they came to the fork in the road. "Old Man Jenkins lives down there."

Mark shook his head and rolled his eyes at her.

"What?" She laughed. "I'm serious. The last visitor who went down there never came out."

"Who told you that?"

"Toad."

Mark laughed. "That figures."

"You mean he made it up?"

Mark shrugged. "Toad never has known the difference between fact and fiction. Did you know he convinced everybody in the town to elect him mayor because he claimed he was kin to some prince of Albania?"

"And people around here believed that?"

"Shoot, they didn't care. None of them wanted to be mayor anyway. He won the election by the unanimous vote of one. His own vote."

Mark navigated the ruts in the road with ease. It had been nine years, he had said, since he'd been here, but he drove it as if it had been yesterday.

"So you think Old Man Jenkins is harmless?" she asked.

"I didn't say that. I think he's probably crazy as a loon, just like most of the people who live up here. When I was a kid, my cousin Spittle and I used to sneak down through the trees and throw rocks at Jenkins' chickens."

"You had a cousin named Spittle?"

"He drooled a lot."

Leah smiled and shook her head in disbelief. "What did Jenkins do to you?"

"He'd shoot at us from his front porch."

"With a gun?"

"No, with a bow and arrow."

"Really?"

"Yeah, he had arrows stuck in all the trees around his property. Never got us, though. Came real close to my cousin's ear one day. Spittle sprayed everyone with the news back home— What the heck is this?"

They had just reached the spot where Bessie's Crick had caused the county road crews to say to hell with it. Cooter's house lay barely visible off to the left in the trees. But parked on the road and in the grass and practically in the creek itself were six or seven vehicles. There were pickups, a station wagon, an old Cadillac skinned down to its primer coat and an ancient Ford tractor.

"What's going on?" Leah asked. "Spencer, wake up, we're here."

The boy sat up and stared sleepily at the congregation of vehicles.

Mark slapped the steering wheel. "Dammit!"

"What's the matter?"

"It's going to be a damned convention, that's what."

"Whose cars are these?" asked Spencer, leaning over the front seat to get a better look.

Mark switched off the engine with a vengeance. "Probably every danged relative in the county."

"Oh, boy!" Spencer jumped out of the car and slammed the door excitedly.

Mark got out and slammed the door, also. His was done with something other than excitement.

Leah got out and closed her door. Gently.

After donning their coats, they began making their way through the bare brush that lay like a tangled web among the thicket of trees. Spencer maneuvered through it like a jackrabbit. Leah and Mark thrashed their way through somewhat less gracefully.

As they neared the clearing, they could hear voices, loud and laughing. Leah's spirits rose with each decibel that rang through the trees. But one glance at Mark's face—even with the reflective sunglasses hiding most of it—told her his reaction was anything but pleased.

"It's going to be fun," she said, taking hold of his arm. "You'll see."

He glanced at her morosely. "An hour with the Beverly Hillbillies is fun. All day with my relatives is not."

She squeezed his arm and laughed. "You old grinch."

Up in front, Spencer called out, "Hey, Pop!"

The screen door slammed open and a swarm of wool-coated figures came flying out into the yard. As Leah and Mark came into the clearing, they saw Pop had picked up Spencer and was swinging him around.

"You're going to break your back, Dad," chided Mark, stepping up to ease Spencer out of Pop's arms and to the ground.

With his hand on his lower back, Pop cranked himself to an upright position. "I'm fit as a fiddle," he grumbled, looking directly at his son. "'Bout time y' got here. We was 'bout to decide you'd run off the road somewheres."

At that, the whole woolly clan jumped in to pump hands, slap backs, kiss cheeks, all yammering at once. Leah felt like an Eskimo trapped in a den of polar bears. But they were friendly. She had to give them that. In fact, she'd never felt so welcome before in her life. And they were complete strangers!

"Land's sake," said Rae Dean, peering at Mark's face. "Would y' look at that, Junior. I'm looking smack dab at myself in them glasses. That's me in there. Land's sake. Elbert, you and LaCinda come over here and get a look at this."

The three visitors from town were quickly pried apart and pulled to various sectors of the den. Pop dragged Spencer off to sit on Cousin Ag's tractor. Some of the men had surrounded Mark and one of them, obviously Spittle, was spraying him with the comings and goings of the past ten years. Leah was taken by the arms and led onto the porch, past an inert Cooter on the couch, through the open screen door and into a tiny kitchen, filled to overflowing with folding chairs, a two-burner stove and some of the sweetest smells Leah had ever smelled. On the counter were pies and cakes, a big slab of ham, a skillet of fried okra, smothered potatoes and something green that Aunt Matty claimed was collards.

Leah was pushed into a chair. "Now you get them boots off and stick those pigs right up here on the oven door," ordered Wilhemina. "Best to leave yore coat on, though. So danged many holes in this place, Cooter could make a wren house out of it."

Leah wasn't yet sure which cousins and aunts and uncles went with which others, but they made it clear from the start that they were all one big happy family. And any friend of Pop Carruthers's kin was as good as kin to them.

"Look at y'!" cried Matty, when Mark came into the kitchen looking for Leah. She grasped his face in her two meaty hands and gave his head a hard shake. "Yur all growed up." She gave him a big smack right on the lips. "And look at y'," she said again, turning him so everyone in the kitchen could get a good look, "ain't he somethin' fine, girls?" She picked up a wool hat and fanned herself. "I swear to Pete, yur gonna have us all steamin' up the windows."

Mark laughed good-naturedly, but Leah thought he looked like a trapped animal.

"Where's that boy of yore's? I bet he's starvin' to death."

"Yeah," said Mark. "The men were kind of wondering when we were going to eat."

Rae Dean puffed up like a mad turkey. "You tell Junior that we'll eat when I say we'll eat and to keep his hands off that shine until after supper. You tell 'im now. Go on. Go tell 'im."

Mark backed out the doorway like an unwanted varmint she was shooing away. "Yes, ma'am," he said, and was not seen for another hour.

THE AFTERNOON TEMPERATURE was still in the thirties, but with so many people stirring around and so many bowls of food, each one passed around like a good piece of juicy gossip, Leah didn't notice. The talk alone was enough to take one's mind off the cold.

It was several hours before they could break away on their own. Mark had a surprise for Spencer. He had brought along a hatchet, and they were going to hunt for a Christmas tree. A real tree.

The three of them, risking a tongue-lashing from Matty Rae, declined another piece of Aunt Bill's buttermilk pie. Mark took the hatchet, and they set off through the trees.

"I love your family, Mark!" Leah said when they were out of earshot.

"Yeah, well, I see Matty Rae's as ripe as ever."

"I'm serious, Mark. I think they're great."

"They never heard of indoor plumbing."

She elbowed him in the side. "You're terrible."

"What about this one?" cried Spencer, darting from one tree to the next, oblivious of Mark's critique of the kinfolk. "This looks pretty good. Oh, but look at this one!"

Mark held the hatchet over one shoulder and took Leah's hand with his free one as they tried to keep up with the frantic dash of an eight-year-old in search of a Christmas tree.

"I think he wants a real tree," marveled Mark.

Leah shook her head and smiled. "What I can't believe is that it took you this long to figure it out."

"Nobody likes my bronze tree."

"Some of us just appreciate the real thing more."

He tightened his grip on her hand and looked at her. Leah Johnson, he realized, was a real thing. There was nothing artificial or shadowy about her. She was real, tangible, warm and living. This, he knew, was what had been missing in his life for so long. Something real to hold on to.

"Abel likes it, though," he mumbled more to himself than to her, still working on the contradictions in his mind.

"Is that what matters, Mark?"

"It has for the past ten years. His opinion has been the most important one to me."

"And now?"

"Now, I don't know anymore. I owe him so much, Leah."

"What do you owe him?"

"My job."

"You could have gotten a job anywhere, Mark. You're smart and talented. Any other company would have seen that as well as Constance Aeronautics."

They walked along silently for a bit. "You know," he said, "it's funny in a way. I sent out applications to all sorts of firms. And I got several offers. But I took this one. The one closest to where I grew up. I wonder why I didn't move farther away."

"Maybe because you really didn't want to leave home. Maybe somewhere inside yourself you knew this was where you belonged."

He stopped walking and dropped the hatchet, then hauled Leah against him. The heat from his body surged into hers, and his hands flattened against her waist and hips. "This is where you belong," he said huskily.

She tried to find her breath. "You think so?"

"I know so."

"Hey, you guys," called Spencer. "Come on. I've found one."

Mark heaved a fatalistic sigh, stooped and picked up the hatchet, then they joined Spencer down the hill. He was standing beside a twenty-foot pine that had a trunk with a diameter of ten inches.

"What do you think?" he asked.

Leah and Mark looked at each other and laughed.

"A little big, Spence," said Mark. "I'm not sure that one would fit in the trunk of the car."

"Oh," he said, disappointed. "I s'pose so."

Mark laid his hand on Spencer's shoulder and led him toward another stand of trees. "Don't worry, we'll find one."

Leah followed behind them, watching them walk together. A week ago, they hadn't been able to find any common ground between them. But now they were arm in arm in search of the perfect Christmas tree.

When she caught up with them, Mark was squatting on his heels before a tree, explaining something to Spencer.

"He says it's a cedar," said Spencer to Leah when she walked up. "What kind, Dad?"

"An atlas cedar."

"Beautiful," said Leah. The tree was about six feet tall and was thick with waxy blue needles. Cones nestled near the ends of each branch.

Mark stood up, still looking at the tree. He was thinking of Pop's conversation with Spencer last week. *Ellie shore did love that tree. Think that was yore granny's all-time favorite.*

"What do you think of this one, Spence?" he asked. "It's nice and fat."

"I love it!" he said. "Don't ya love it, Leah?"

"I do," she said with a smile. "I think it's just perfect." She caught Mark's eyes and said quietly. "I don't think I've ever seen a more beautiful tree."

His eyes were as soft as the cedar blue as he looked at her and said, "Neither have I."

"Come on," urged Spencer. "Let's hurry and cut it."

Mark laughed. "It's not going to run away, Spence. But, okay, you guys stand back now."

Leah reached for Spencer and pulled him with her while Mark slipped off his jacket and picked up the hatchet. He hefted it until the weight was distributed properly, then raised it high, swinging it in an arc until it struck soundly against the trunk of the tree. Splinters of wood flew into the air. Time and time again he struck until the tree leaned precariously.

"I'll catch it!" cried Spencer.

"No, no," said Leah, holding him back. "Just let it fall."

With the final blow, the tree toppled over onto the hard frozen earth. Mark set down the hatchet and slipped on his jacket, while Leah and Spencer ran over and tried to lift the tree.

"I'll have to drag it," said Mark.

"Won't it hurt , Dad?"

"Me? Are you kidding?"

"No, I mean the tree."

"Nah, won't hurt a thing." He reached down and wrapped his hand around the trunk, lifting it. He glanced at Leah. "Cooter's hot rum sounds good about now."

Leah picked up the hatchet. "Are you sure you don't want help with that?"

"Me, Tarzan," Mark said, thumping his chest. "Boy. Lead way to village."

"Follow me!" Spencer said, running on ahead.

Leah fell in step with Mark and he said, "You can call me Bwana."

She laughed. "So how does it feel, Bwana, being a country boy again?"

"Surprisingly good." He shifted the trunk to his other hand.

"Uh-huh," she goaded when he shifted the weight of the tree. "Gotten soft, living in the city, have you?"

He grinned lasciviously. "Only in certain areas."

She stooped and pulled up some frozen blades of grass and threw them at him.

THE MEN WERE MOVING into a stupor from the mounds of food and the homemade shine. The women's talk had tapered to an easy rhythm that matched the dunk of a plate in dishwater and the swish of a towel around a bowl.

Spencer and the young cousins were off scaring up trouble in the tool shed.

Cooter was sleeping off all the excitement on the front porch, so Pop reached for the rifle by the door. "Wanna come?"

Mark let the front legs of his chair drop to the porch floor. "Okay."

The sky was turning to all sorts of colors, nothing brilliant or showy, just an afternoon blend that rested easy on the eyes. The grass lay limp against the wet ground.

The two men walked silently beside each other. They passed through a dry creek bed, skirted the edge of a thicket of tall, skinny pines, then slogged through wet rye grass. Pop sat down on a log and pulled a cigar from his pocket. He stuck it in his mouth, unlit. Mark propped one foot on the log and pulled a pine cone from a tree.

"So."

Mark contemplated the perfectly shaped cone in his hand.

"You about ready to come home?"

The old man spit on the tail of his shirt and rubbed a spot on the gun barrel. "Home?"

"Yes."

"Cooter seems to enjoy my company."

Mark tossed the pine cone into the brown needles that blanketed the ground. "Cooter won't even know you're gone for a week. Today's activities won't catch up with him for a month."

"Been nice and quiet-like here the past couple days."

Mark started pulling needles from a branch. "Spencer misses you."

"Miss him, too."

"I could use some help putting up that cedar I cut today."

"Y' need to cut off a couple inches on that trunk. Y' always gotta do that."

I know that, he started to say. Instead, he said, "Yes, sir."

"And make sure y' put a pinch of sugar in the water."

Mark finished shredding the branch. "Yes, sir."

"Ellie always put a pinch of sugar in cut flowers, too. A little sweetenin' goes a long way, she'd always say. I 'member the time . . ." The thought trailed off into the still afternoon light.

Mark shifted, taking his left foot from the log and propping up his right.

"That neighbor of yore's still mad 'bout that dog?"

"He hasn't said anything."

Pop picked up the rifle and sighted down it. He laid it back in his lap and looked at Mark. "You still mad?"

Mark shook his head.

"Spencer, he said you was mad as a wet hornet that I took off."

"I was worried."

"Been takin' care of myself for a long time, son."

"I know that. But Spencer said something about you living under some bridge."

"Thought about it. Tried it for one night. It wasn't near as much fun as fellowship with Cooter."

Mark thought that was debatable, but he didn't say so. "It was a fool thing to do, Dad, running off like that. Anything could have happened."

"I ain't livin' in any old folks' home."

"It was a retirement home, Pop."

"Well, I ain't going there. Ain't retirin' neither."

"Look," Mark said, ripping off another handful of needles. "It was a mistake. I was wrong. Is that what you want to hear?"

Pop lifted the rifle and aimed. Mark, his nerves already shot, jerked at the loud crack.

"Go fetch me that squirrel, will y', son?"

Mark threw the needles to the ground and stepped over the log. He walked about thirty yards and picked up the dead squirrel, carried it back and dropped it at his father's feet.

"That girl talk y' into comin' up here to get me?"

"She had something to do with it."

"She's a dandy one. Reminds me a bunch of Ellie. Same softness inside her. Yore mama had a good heart."

"Yes, sir. I know that."

"She shore thought the world of you. She knew y' was different from the rest of us. Knew she had to let y' go, even though it near broke her heart."

Mark looked out over the fallow field beyond the trees. "I want you to come home, Pop. Not for Spencer. Not because of Leah."

Pop stuffed the cigar into his pocket and looked at his son. Waiting.

"*I* want you to come, Dad."

With great effort, Pop stood up, lifting the squirrel with him. With dead animal hanging from one hand and rifle hanging from the other, he looked at Mark and said, "Y' probably could use some help with that tree." He turned toward the house. "Now, ole Jasper, y' 'member him? He always thought Christmas just wadn't Christmas without a goose. But he liked those danged noisy Canadian kind. Now, I can't rightly imagine how anybody could . . ."

Mark walked beside his father, only half-listening, but feeling really good inside. Better than he'd felt in a long, long time.

Chapter Twelve

Mark picked up two mugs of hot rum and handed one to Leah. He leaned toward her. "Come with me," he whispered.

She caught the secret smile that played around his lips before he turned and headed for the door. Holding both hands around the mug for warmth, she followed him onto the porch. "Where are we going?"

He stepped down into the yard. "Come on, I want to show you something."

The sky was almost white beneath the afternoon sun, with only a slim band of color along the western horizon. The frozen grass had thawed until droplets of water clung to the tips of each blade.

Mark waited for her to catch up. Then he took her hand.

She laughed. "Where are you taking me, Tarzan?"

"Bwana, remember? And I'm taking you someplace warm."

She let him lead her across the cold wet grass, past a rusted tin shed that was falling in on a stack of dry wooden planks. They walked through a small stand of trees and came out where a branch of the creek had made an icy rivulet through the grass. Mark took both their cups and jumped across. After setting the cups on the ground, he reached for Leah and, with his hands around her waist, lifted her over. Once on the other side, they picked up their cups and climbed a small hill.

Down below lay a slow-moving creek. It took a meandering course through the pasture and into the woods beyond.

"That's Lindy Creek. Our house was back in those woods."

"Is it still there?"

"No. A few years back, a bad storm came through. Floods, high winds. That was the end of the old place."

"Were you able to save anything?"

He shook his head. "I didn't even come up here to see the damage. Pop told me about it. At the time, my thought was good riddance."

"Is that when Pop came to live with you?"

"He moved in with Matty Rae and her husband, Bubba, for a while. I finally convinced him to come join civilization."

They came to another shed, this one standing upright and still intact. If it had once worn paint, the paint had long since eroded away. The gray weathered planks were dotted with knotholes, and near the ground the bottoms of the boards had been eaten away by rot or termites.

Mark led her around the front of the shed and pushed open the door. It caught a couple of times, but with pressure it opened on rusted hinges.

It was dark inside. Leah hung back. "Is it safe?"

"Oh, sure. We might stir up a few field mice, but that doesn't scare you, does it?"

"Yes."

He laughed, but then he saw the look of terror on her face, he said, "Look, stay here a minute. I'll open it up." He walked into the dark shed and she heard the creak of hinges. Light soon flooded the interior, so she peeked her head around the door. Mark was going around the perimeter, opening windows to let in the light. She could see now that it wasn't as frightening inside as she had imagined. A few bales of old hay had busted open and were strewn around on one side. A rusted horse bit lay on the dirt floor.

"Was this a horse barn?"

"Cooter and Pop kept some mules in here at one time. And Pop used to store fresh baled hay in here to sell. Come on in. It's harmless."

Leah stepped in and scanned the floor. "I don't see any mice."

"Nah," he said. "We've scared them off by now."

She looked up at the ceiling.

"No bats, either, Leah." He came over and took her hand.

"What about snakes?"

"Too cold for them." He wrapped his arm around her shoulder. "Might be a dragon or two, though, so you'd better stick close."

"Be serious. I'm not used to this sort of thing."

"Never spent much time in barns?"

"Never."

He slowly surveyed the open space. "This was one of the best parts of growing up."

"A barn?"

He turned toward her and lowered his arm to her waist. With his free hand, he brushed the loose strands of hair away from her face. His voice, when he spoke, was deep and warm. "You'd be amazed at the fun you can have in a barn."

"Oh, yeah?" she asked breathlessly, her knees weakening.

"Yeah," he said softly, then smiled. "You can throw hay down on people from the loft." His fingertip followed the arch of her eyebrow. "You can swing from the pulley rope." The finger slid down the bridge of her nose. "You can climb on the rafters." It traced the outline of her mouth. "You can find all sorts of old junk to collect." It dropped over her chin and down her neck. "Barns are lots of fun." His head bent low and his mouth lightly brushed against hers, his tongue barely touching her upper lip.

"I—I see what you mean," she whispered against his mouth.

His thumb replaced his mouth against her lips, and he looked down at her with a half smile. "Let me show you my favorite hiding place."

Too breathless to answer, she let him lead her toward a ladder that was fixed against the wall.

"I'll go first," he said and began to climb up. "Wow," he said when he reached the top. "I can't believe it."

"What?" she asked fearfully, envisioning the skeletal remains of one of the cousins. "What's up there?"

"Some of my old junk. I can't believe it's still up here."

Gathering strength, she climbed up and poked her head above the loft. A few dusty bales of hay sat around the room like furniture, and several boxes were filled with what looked like pieces of rusted car parts and old metal signs.

Leah climbed all the way up and walked over to where Mark was kneeling down, rummaging through one of the boxes. "This is your stuff?"

"Yes, can you believe it? Of course, I don't know why I thought it wouldn't be here. I can't imagine Cooter ever coming out here to clean this place up."

"Are these off cars?"

"Yeah, there's—or there *was* a junkyard up the road a bit. I used to find all sorts of motors and crankshafts and flywheels. Built some great gizmos out of them."

"Did you spend much time up here?"

Mark reached over and opened the loft door. The afternoon sun flooded into the small room. "Yeah. When Pop didn't have me working, I was usually up here. Did my homework here, too. If I tried to study in the house, Pop would always bug me. He'd ask me if I wouldn't rather stretch some fence wire. Or wouldn't I rather go hunt up a possum for supper? It was always something. He couldn't understand how I could enjoy all that book learning. So this was the only place I could get some peace and quiet."

Now that Leah knew the area was devoid of rodents and skeletons, she started to relax. The sun felt good on her face as it streamed through the rectangular opening. The fields beyond lay fallow and brown under the winter sky. "What a great place to grow up," she said wistfully.

Mark's gaze followed hers over the fields. "Funny," he mused, "how it seemed like a trap for so many years. Like a sinkhole out of which I couldn't seem to crawl." He shook his head and looked at her. "You make me see it all differently, Leah. It's like a whole new way of looking at my past."

She smiled softly. "I'm glad, Mark." Looking into his face and eyes, she felt as if she was looking at a fertile field, rich in things you couldn't see. Solid and good. *I think I love you,* she wanted to say. *This is crazy, but I really think I love you.*

"Are you cold?" he asked.

"No."

"You're shivering."

She hadn't realized. She didn't feel the least bit cold.

He reached out with his hand and wrapped his fingers around her arm. "Come here."

She came over and sat down next to him. His legs were stretched out in front of him, his back against the wall. He scooped up her legs beneath the knees and draped them over his. His arm looped around her waist, supporting her.

"I'll keep you warm," he said, leaning against the wall and pulling her more tightly against him. His free hand lay over her legs.

They sat this way for a while, just looking out the door and watching the sun slide down the blue-white sky into a slim band of coral.

"You know," he finally said, "I never could be the man Angela wanted me to be. I don't think I realized that until just now."

"What kind of man did she want you to be?"

"A man of polish. Stature. Certainly not some poor white trash from the hills."

"You're not trash."

He smiled at her. "No, I'm not. But I thought I was. I let her convince me that, without her, that was all I would ever be." A dry chuckle came from his throat. "The first night I met her was at a party Abel had thrown in her honor. I had known her for exactly an hour when she led me into her dark bedroom and started unbuttoning my shirt."

"You're kidding!"

"No, I'm not. She was a fast mover. She had set her sights on me and she was moving in for the kill."

Leah turned her head and looked at him. "Can't say that I blame her. She liked what she saw."

Mark absently lifted a strand of her hair and let it run through his fingers. He stared at it, but he was seeing something long past. "She told me I turned her on. Said she liked wild boys like me. With mountain fire in their blood, I think she called it." He shook his head. "I can't believe I'm talking to you about this."

Leah rested her hand against his chest. "I want you to talk to me."

His hand moved up her thigh, slowly, until it reached the side of her hip.

He chuckled again, this time in a self-mocking tone. "That—that mountain fire was the first thing she tried to drive out of me when we were married. Claimed a man who was raised on the right side of the tracks didn't behave like that in bed."

Something stirred within her and at the spot where his hand rested against her hip. The nerve endings burned as if by fire. Mountain fire. "Like what?" she managed to ask.

His eyes had become surprisingly vulnerable, as if he was issuing a warning and fully expected to be censured. "She decided she wanted finesse. That was what a man of substance was supposed to have. Finesse. She tried to mold me into the kind of lover I was supposed to be, but—well, I guess I never stacked up."

"And that bothers you?" she asked, painfully aware that there was a very real possibility that he still loved his wife.

"Not that I didn't meet her qualifications as a lover."

Leah wanted to breathe a sigh of relief, but she still felt unsure. "Then what?"

He looked at her with eyes that were as deep as a summer sky, burning a path through her flesh. His voice, when he spoke, was low and full of raw energy. "That I won't meet yours."

Her breath ceased and she could only stare at him for a long time. Finally she spoke. "I don't know that I have any expectations, Mark. I don't have any standard of measurement."

"I guess I just wanted you to know."

"Know what?"

"That I'm from this side of the tracks. What I am."

"I know who you are."

His hand slid from the front of her thigh up over her abdomen where it stopped. "I'm a country boy," he said, lowering her to the floor as he came over on top of her. "I just do it like we did it back here on the mountain."

"Good," she said, frantically searching for her breath. "I love the country."

"There isn't much finesse to it."

The pain of her own past had never left her. It was always, always there. "I've had finesse, Mark," she said quietly. "It doesn't last."

His gaze traveled slowly over her face and neck, studying the sadness in her eyes, wanting to make it go away at any cost to himself, wanting to give everything for the first time in his life.

His gaze dropped to her chest, heating every square inch with eyes that seemed to strip her naked. "I can't believe I'm here with you like this. Talking to you like this. I've—I've never been this open with anyone before."

"I've never had anyone be open with me, honest with me before."

"I want to give you what you need, Leah. And I know women like to talk about things like this, but I'm not sure I know how."

Her hands came up to his chest, spreading the lapels of his leather coat. Her fingers began slowly working the buttons loose on his shirt. She smiled seductively and ran her hand along the exposed expanse of skin beneath his shirt. "You mountain boys didn't talk about it much?"

His breath seemed to draw her in, and his eyes blazed over her like the sun over the desert. "No," he answered huskily. "We were too busy doing it in the hay loft to talk about it."

You're going to fall, Leah. You're going to tumble down this mountain and you're going to end up needing him. Just like all the others.

No. Not like all the others. Not this time.

She pressed small kisses against his neck and chest. "Doing what?" she breathed against his flesh.

His hand moved along her leg, coming to rest at the junction of her inner thighs. His mouth dropped down to her neck, then slid like a slow-moving creek up to her ear. "This, Leah." His hand began to knead her body, while his tongue worked magic against the side of her neck. "This."

She moaned softly against his chest. "It's been a long time, Mark."

"For me, too," he whispered. "Tell me what you want, Leah."

He slowly lowered the zipper on her jeans, and his hand snaked inside. She tried to pull his jacket from his arms, but he wouldn't let go of her body long enough to take it off.

"Mark."

He sat up and ripped the jacket from his arms, throwing it onto one of the boxes. The flannel shirt came next. Leah was sitting up, too, trying to pull her sweater over her head. Mark reached over to help her. Goose bumps ran across her flesh, but his hands sent a flood of warmth into her skin.

Wrapping his arms around her, she fell back, and his mouth covered her breast, sending arrows of fire coursing through her body. With his free hand, he tugged at her jeans, sliding them down over her hips and legs. He pressed into her, and she grasped his jean-clad hips.

She couldn't get enough of him, fast enough.

"Do you want finesse?" he whispered harshly against her mouth, his lower body pressing her into the floor.

"No." She grasped the back of his head, her fingers woven through his hair. "I want you."

Letting go of her, he stood up and took off his jeans and tossed them with the other clothes.

He came back to her, wrapping his body over and around her. "Are you cold?" he asked, pressing his body into hers, his mouth forming the words onto her lips, praying she would say no, praying that nothing would end this moment of torturous bliss.

"No," she whispered, arching her body as his heat rushed through her. "I—I'm..."

"Hot," he moaned against her mouth. "Hot," he whispered as he grasped her bare hips with his hand and dragged her tightly against him, his body surging with hers, finding a home.

The late afternoon sun spilled through the rectangular opening, warming the sprinkling of dry hay, the boxes of childhood memories and the man and woman who clung to each other, desperately searching for a past, a present and a future. Together.

Chapter Thirteen

Mark set the file on Abel's desk. "Well, here it is."

Abel opened the file and scanned the scale drawings. "It looks good. What about costs?"

"I cut all I could. It's not going to be a cheap plane. They have to know that."

"We're bidding against tough competition."

"I know that, Abel."

"I want this contract, Mark."

Mark's eyes narrowed on his father-in-law. He pulled up a chair and sat down, leaning his forearms on the desk across from him. "What is this, Abel?"

"What is what?" the older man growled.

Mark reached over and flipped the file closed. "It's not this damn bid that's bugging you. So why don't you tell me what it is."

It had been building for over a week now, this tension between them. Ever since the night Spencer yelled at Abel. Or maybe it started the night of the dinner party, when Leah came to the door. Maybe it had been going on for ten years, and Mark had just been too stupid to see it. Whenever it had begun, it was now time to get it out in the open.

"I have been waiting for your apology," said Abel, scowling across the wide expanse of desk.

"My apology?"

"For Spencer's behavior the other night. For your behavior."

"Spencer's getting to be a big boy, Abel. He can do his own apologizing."

A flush was creeping over the older man's neck and onto his lower jaw. "His behavior was inexcusable."

"He felt that you maligned his grandfather."

"*I* am his grandfather!"

"So is Pop, Abel." Mark stared at his hands clasped on the desk. "They're real close."

"It isn't healthy. You know that."

Mark glanced up. "In what way?"

Abel was rapidly losing patience. He had always been a man who expected the rest of the world to get his meaning immediately and, if not, to keep quiet about it. He was not a man to tolerate debate. "He will fill his head with all sorts of ideas and notions. He's from the mountain, Mark. Is that the way you want Spencer to grow up?"

A month ago—even two weeks ago—Mark knew what his answer would have been. But nothing was the same anymore. Leah had changed everything.

"Well, is it?"

"There are things I want Spencer to have," Mark said carefully. "Things I didn't have. But there is something called values." He shook his head. "I know now that they have very little to do with money. Or with living on the right side of the tracks."

Abel's scowl deepened. "What on earth are you talking about?"

Mark couldn't expect him to understand. He knew that. He had forced himself to live solely in Abel's world, and by Abel's rules, and with Abel's values. His own had been swept under the rug a long time ago.

"I'm talking about good things in life, Abel. I'm talking about things that money can't buy. I didn't have such a bad childhood. I realize that now. I had two parents who loved me. They loved me so much they let me grow away from them."

"You were destined to be better than they were," grumbled Abel.

"Not better." Mark shook his head. "Not better, Abel. Only different. But what happened is that, in pursuit of—" he waved his arm to encompass the richly paneled office "—of all this, I forgot about all the good things they gave me."

Abel's eyes were narrowed on Mark's face, and he said, "What is the matter with you? What has happened to you? Is it Angela? Ever since she left you,

you've been different. Oh, don't think I haven't noticed. You miss her, don't you?''

Mark's small smile was for all the world's folly. His
own. And especially Abel's.

"No," he said carefully. "I don't miss her. I never
loved her, Abel."

The red flush moved farther up the older man's
face. "You married my daughter. I gave her to you.
She left you." He sniffed. "I thought at the time she
was a fool."

"I thought I loved her, Abel. She represented
everything I never had. She was—hell, she was sophisticated, gorgeous, well-to-do." Mark leaned on
his elbows and stared at his father-in-law. "She was
your daughter. She was my ticket."

Abel sat back in his chair and laced his fingers
across his stomach. "And this is where you expect me
to jump up and deck you, right? Where you expect
me to stand up and defend my daughter's honor?"

Mark said nothing. He just studied the man from
the other side of the desk.

"Well, I won't," said Abel, with a casual tone.
"That's what someone from your neck of the woods
might do. But that's the big difference, you see. We
are civilized. We know that things are done, relationships are forged that have little to do with what's right
or wrong, good or bad. They serve a purpose, that is
all. Your marriage to Angela served a purpose. For
me. And for you. I'm not the least bit shocked that

you did not love her. I didn't much care for her mother, either. That, too, was an arrangement. Purely business."

This, thought Mark, was the man he had emulated for the past ten years. This was what he strove to become.

No more. "I'm looking for something more in life, Abel."

"Like what?"

He shrugged. "A family life. Love. Something with substance."

Abel sat very still, his fingers still clenched together over his stomach. "It's that girl, isn't it? That piano teacher."

Mark nodded. "That's the one."

"You can't be serious."

"I'm dead serious."

"She is some sort of charity worker, Mark. She will do nothing for your career."

"*My* career, Abel? Or the one *you've* created?"

It took a minute for the meaning of that to soak in. "What are you saying?" Abel hesitated again. "That—that you're quitting the firm?"

"That's up to you, I guess."

Abel leaned forward with his hands flattened against the desk, his voice harsh and low. "This does not make sense. What the hell do you think you're doing?"

"I'm trying to put my life on track," said Mark. "I'm trying to do that before it's too late."

"And you think that hanging around this girl and throwing away ten years of work is going to help you do that?"

"First of all, Abel, I have no intention of hanging around her. I'm going to ask her to marry me." He ignored the shocked bluster that came from Abel's throat. "Secondly, I'm not throwing away my career. Only you can do that. I like what I do. I find great satisfaction in it. But I know now it's not the end all to my life."

"If you married that girl, how could you possibly expect her to fit in to our social arena?"

Mark chuckled. "Abel, that girl—as you call her—was raised with more money than you and I and every employee in this company put together has. Believe me, she knows her way around the civilized set. But I have no intention of dragging her to any of those intensely boring social events you enjoy so much. They're a drag, Abel. I've hated them for ten years. I hate golf, did you know that? The idea of knocking a little white ball around a cow pasture is absurd. I did it, all of it, because you wanted me to. That's the only reason."

Abel's chin shot forward. "You should have said something before."

"You're right. I should have. But I didn't have the guts."

Abel shook his head. "I cannot accept this. No, I simply cannot."

Mark nodded slowly and stood up. "Then I'm sorry, Abel. You've got a great company here. I'll miss that."

"You'll never find anyone who will mold you the way I have."

"No, you're right there. But I'm through being molded. I know now who I am, where I came from and where I want to go."

"You won't find another job."

Mark scoffed at that. "Come on, Abel. I graduated with honors. I've got ten years of experience. I'll find another job."

"Not at this salary. Not at this position."

Mark shrugged. "You're probably right there. But, you see, I don't care. I've made enough money that I could retire, if I wanted to. If I want to work, I'll find a job." He turned and walked to the door.

His hand was on the knob when Abel said, "I suppose Spencer will forget all about me."

Mark turned around slowly. "That, again, is up to you."

"He said he hated me."

"He doesn't hate you. He doesn't hate anybody. All Spencer wants is to be loved. He's had too little of it in his life. He wants a family. He wants to feel secure."

Mark waited, watching the strange play of emotions that crossed Abel's face. When he spoke, it was with difficulty. "I might come now and then to check on his progress at the piano."

Abel's face and body were as stiff and inflexible as iron behind the desk. But inside, Mark saw the bent man. "That would be fine, Abel." He turned once more and reached for the doorknob.

"We'd have to work out different terms, you know."

Mark kept his back to the man to hide the tentative smile that was starting to form. "Terms?"

Abel cleared his throat. "If you stayed on."

Mark forced the smile away and turned around. He kept his face blank, his expression noncommittal, his voice silent.

"What I mean," grumbled Abel, "is that there would have to be some adjustments. I might find someone else to entertain clients with me, to present bids." The chin jutted out once more in challenge. "What do you think of that?"

"All I want to do, Abel, is design. That's all I've ever wanted to do. I hate working up bids and dealing with the Pentagon brass and the presidents of these airline companies. I want to design."

"I might not be able to pay you as much."

Mark retained the blank look, waiting patiently, refusing to give an inch.

Abel coughed and sputtered. "Oh, to hell with it," he mumbled. "If you want to stay, stay. I suppose you'll be wanting some time off for some sort of—of honeymoon, or something."

Mark finally let the smile slide across his face.

Abel saw the smile and couldn't resist one more dig. "Of course, you're assuming this girl is going to want to marry you."

"Well, y' know somethin', Abel," Mark said with a smile, "us mountain boys have got us a way with the girls. Yep, they just plum can't resist us."

THE BELL ABOVE THE DOOR clanged, and the memories of this place flooded his mind once more. But this time, the activities before him held his attention. It was a moment in time. In the present. There was no room for painful memories.

Lilla DeHaven stood behind the counter, tallying up the day's accounts. Spencer was sitting on the counter, eating a piece of cake. Leah and Pop were holding a friendly argument over how the hats should be organized, Leah insisting that they be lined up by head size and Pop contending that they be set up alphabetically, according to whose head they'd fit.

"Now this un'd be just right for Elbert's head. And E shore as tarnation comes before F."

"This is not here because it will fit somebody with the initial F, Pop—"

"Freddy Jessup."

"Freddy," she said. "It's here because it's a size medium. That one you say is for Elbert is a large. Medium comes before large."

Mark jiggled the door to make the bell ring again. Finally everyone looked up. "Hello."

The greetings began with Spencer jumping down from the counter and running up to give him a hug. Icing from the boy's fingers stuck to his father's coat sleeve.

From behind the counter, Lilla gave Mark a suspicious look, as if she wondered briefly if she should keep her eye on him.

"I'm not going to pull the legs out from under the tables," Mark said, and she went back to her figures.

Leah came over and stood on tiptoes to give him a kiss. He wrapped his arms around her and deepened the kiss.

"You two are _onna scare away the customers," said Pop from across the room. "Why, I never seen such carrying on."

Mark reluctantly dragged his mouth away from hers and looked over the top of her head. The three of them were looking at Mark and Leah as if they'd never seen anybody kiss before.

Mark bent down and whispered, "Let's get out of here."

She giggled. "I'm working, Mark."

"Just for a few minutes. Please."

The desperation in his voice matched the one in her body. She glanced at Lilla. "Can you spare me for a few minutes?"

Lilla scowled. "What for?"

Mark answered. "I need to talk to Leah in private. Just for a little while."

"I reckon."

Spencer ran up to the counter. "Pop and I can help you out, Lilla."

She snorted and laid her hand on the top of Spencer's blond head. "You, maybe." She glanced at Pop. "But that old coot'll have this place in a shambles before y' can say cat scratch fever."

"Cat scratch fever," said Spencer. "Nope, Pop hasn't messed up anything yet."

Lilla snorted again.

Mark and Leah didn't wait for any more. Leah slipped on her coat and they were out the door, the clang of the bell lost on the cold wintry day.

They were inside her house within seconds. She barely had the door closed and locked before Mark had her in his arms. His hands worked quickly at the buttons on her coat. "I told Abel that you couldn't resist me." His mouth was over her, urgently tasting, wanting to devour. He pulled her arms from the coat sleeves. His voice was a ragged groan against her face. "Can you?" he breathed huskily. "Can you resist me?"

Leah tried to catch her breath. Her hands flattened against his chest, but he gave her no time or will to resist anything. She pressed herself against him, whispering against his mouth. "No. I can't resist you."

He grasped the back of her head with one hand and her hips with another. His mouth raked a fiery path to her temple. "I want more, Leah."

"More?" she whispered breathlessly. Her heart was pounding next to his. Her body begged for his touch. "I don't—"

He grasped her arms and held her in front of him, his chest rising and falling as he stared at her. "This isn't enough."

It was all happening so fast. Her need for him every time he was near. This rush of excitement that flooded through her. They couldn't keep their hands off each other. But now he was holding her back, wanting something more. Past hurts crashed in on her, pushing reality into her realm of vision. She laid her hands against his chest, formed a tentative smile and forced a light tone she didn't feel. "I'm not into anything kinky, Mark."

He pulled her to him and laughed against the top of her head. "Be serious. Don't you know, I can't stand this, Leah. You living here."

She grew still in his arms, her pulse pounding against his chest and in her neck. "It bothers you?"

"Yes."

"I'm sorry."

He, too, grew quiet, then he pulled back and looked down at her, frowning. "No, no." He shook his head. "You've got it wrong. I didn't mean it like that. I mean I can't stand you being here and me being way across town."

She had never known this kind of love before. This all-consuming need to be a part of someone's life. Mark had showed her everything she had ever imagined love could be. But there was always a chance that it could end. The possibility of pain was always on the horizon. She wanted to be serious, but she couldn't. If this were all some sort of joke or some kind of interlude, she wasn't going to take it too seriously.

She tried another smile. "Are you wanting to move in?"

Mark heaved an impatient sigh and stared down at the floor between them. "I am really botching this thing up." He shook his head, but kept his eyes cast downward. "I've never proposed to anyone before. Angela was the one who—"

"Proposed?" She stared at him as his head slowly came up. No, it wasn't real. Good things did not often come her way. She had been hurt too many times to easily accept this as real.

He smiled at her. "Yes. That's what I'm trying to do." He laid his hand against her face and, with his thumb, gently stroked away the frown. "I want you to marry me, Leah. I want you to be my wife."

She continued to stare at him, wanting to believe but so afraid that if she did, the moment would vanish like a flash of lightning before her eyes.

"Leah?" Mark held her face between both hands. "Are you in there?"

"Yes."

He frowned, studying her face until the realization slowly sunk in. He finally understood. "I'm not passing out empty promises, Leah. I love you. I really do. I've never felt this way in my life."

Her lips parted to speak, but she held the words in.

"Please talk to me," he whispered. "Please tell me that you love me, too."

She swallowed hard. "I do, Mark. You—you've made me feel things I've never felt before."

"Then what's the problem? Is it me? Is it Spencer? What is it?"

Tears welled up in her eyes, and he pulled her to his chest, holding her head and making her feel so secure and safe. "It's not Spencer, Mark. I love your son. I love your whole family."

"It's me, then?" he said quietly above her head.

"Yes."

He grew very still, his heart the only thing within him that did not cease to function.

"I love you so much," she said, still leaning into him, aware of the rigid stillness that had taken hold of his body. "And the way you treat me, the way you make love to me—I've never felt this kind of love from anyone. I was a burden to my parents. And for other guys, well—I was a ticket to their future or I was a new kick, a good time—I don't know. I was never important to anyone."

"You're very important to me, Leah. You've changed my life. You've made me real again. You've given me the best gift anyone could ever give."

"I'm used to people needing me for things," she said. "But once—once I start needing them . . ."

Mark pulled back and held her head. "You can need me all you want, Leah. I'm not going to turn away from that. Please don't be afraid of needing me the way I need you. I'll never let you fall."

The truth came to her then, standing before him and looking into his face. The truth was that life was a risk. Nothing was ever final, ever inevitable. But to know that someone needed you and to realize that you needed him and could depend on him for as long as life allowed it was worth all the hurt and loneliness and heartbreak that might eventually come your way. Mark loved her. And she loved him. And if they were very, very lucky, they would be able to share a long life together. For that, it was worth all the risk in the world.

"I love you, Mark."

He smiled so gently at her and with so much love, she wondered if she could ever capture it all and contain it.

"But you haven't answered my question," he said.

All hesitation was gone. All fears of empty promises. "I'll marry you, Mark. I'd love to be your wife."

He clutched her to him and rocked her in his arms. "God, I can't believe it. I feel like a kid again, Leah. I feel like putting bows and ribbons all over you and setting you under the tree, just so I can open you up on Christmas morning."

She smiled and hugged him tightly. "You might open me up and decide you want to trade me in for a different model."

"Never. You're the best. The best gift anyone could ever want."

A cat came up and rubbed against Mark's leg. He looked down. "I suppose—which one is this?"

"Gopher."

"I suppose Gopher and Brenda are going to want to sleep at the foot of our bed."

She kissed the front of his shirt and ran her hand down over his hips. "I don't know," she said seductively. "Might be kind of a rough night's sleep. If you know what I mean."

He moaned low in his throat and pulled her into the crook of his body. "Maybe they'd better sleep with Spencer, then. Or Pop."

She lifted her fingers to the top button of his shirt and worked it loose. Her fingernail lightly raked across the exposed expanse of chest. She smiled up at him. "I think that's a great idea."

Chapter Fourteen

Mark came up behind her and looped his arms around her waist. His mouth was next to her ear. "I don't know which is riper," he whispered. "All my unwashed cousins or Junior's sour mash. Look at them," he said staring over the top of her head. "They act like they're at Disney World."

Although he sounded happy, Leah could tell by his voice that Mark was a bit overwhelmed by the big event. Even she had to admit, it was one full Christmas Day.

First, there were all the packages to open. Wrapping paper and ribbons and bows were strewn around so haphazardly, there was barely room to walk.

Everyone had to keep dodging Spencer's remote control race car as it darted in and out of the crowd.

Matty Rae moved through the house like a dust devil, hollering orders to whomever was in earshot.

Rae Dean and LaCinda had a good time clanging pots and pans in Mark's kitchen. They couldn't stop talking about it.

"Have you ever seen anything like it? I swear, we could feed the entire county outa this kitchen. And look at this here thing." They punched the buttons on the microwave and the dishwasher, delighting at all the appliances running at once.

Elbert and Junior and Bubba were tossing back the sour mash and studying the bronze sculpture in the living room, while all the kids used it as a fort, sitting in the center of it, playing with their toys.

"Looks like somebody's mouth," said Junior. "Rae Dean's."

"Nope," mused Elbert. "It's an airplane. You can tell it right off. Look at the way it goes up like that. Yep. That's what it is."

"Looks like a cow pattie to me," said Bubba and, with that comment, they all went back to the serious business of drinking.

Cooter had found himself a place on the couch this morning and, last time Leah looked, he was still there, wrapping paper piling up around him like snow.

It had been Spencer's idea to make the day a family affair. Pop and Leah had enthusiastically supported it. And Mark, being outnumbered, had said okay, fine.

The wedding had taken place only three days ago, but they had both agreed that the honeymoon would be put off until after Christmas. Pop, under Clara's watchful eye, would stay with Spencer while Leah and Mark were gone.

"Chow time," hollered Matty Rae. "Junior, you and Bubba get on over here and leave that sauce alone. We're gonna have to tie y' to yore chairs to keep y' from fallin' out." She looked around for the rest of the crowd. "Where are all the young 'uns? Y'all better git on down here if y' wanna eat! You two lovebirds sit here at this end of the table."

For ten years, Mark had put up with Abel telling him where to sit and what to say and do. Now, he realized, for the next twenty years he was probably going to have to put up with Matty Rae.

He grinned at Leah and sat down next to her at the table. "Come on, Spencer," he said. "You kids sit right along here."

"Not there," boomed Matty Rae. "No, sirree. I want 'em down at that end where I can keep an eye on 'em and whack 'em good with a spoon if they get outa line."

Mark shrugged at Spencer and whispered, "I suggest you behave yourself, son."

Beneath the table, Leah reached for Mark's hand. It had been the happiest three days of her life. Living with him and with Spencer and Pop. They were a family now. Something she had wanted all her life. It was a precious gift, she realized, one she would never take for granted. She had it all. A loving husband. A wonderful son. A fun-loving father. And enough eccentric relatives to start her own carnival.

She smiled at Mark, and he couldn't resist leaning over to give her a kiss.

"Lawd a mercy!" said LaCinda. "You two are gonna give Elbert here ideas."

Elbert took another swig of Junior's mash and reached for the plate of turkey. The only idea he had was to grab enough grub before somebody else did.

"Where you two goin' for your honeymoonin', anyways?" asked Rae Dean.

"Somewhere quiet." Mark laughed.

"Well, land's sake," said LaCinda. "Y'all oughta come up to the mountain then. It's plenty quiet up there. We could cook for y' and—"

"Now, hold on, there," said Pop. "These two have got plans of their own. They're goin' somewheres on their own. Not city. Not mountain. Someplace that's jest theirs." He looked over at Leah and Mark. "Right?"

They both smiled, and Mark lifted his glass in toast. "That's right, Pop. Just ours."

"This is the best Christmas ever!" cried Spencer, smiling around the long table at his huge family. They all lifted their glasses in agreement.

"The best ever," said Mark, looking at his father, and his son, and all his relatives. He looked at Leah and clinked his glass against hers. "The very best."

The turkey and potatoes and stuffing and countless other bowls of vegetables and breads were gone. The plates of cakes and pies had taken center stage on the table. Matty Rae was standing at the head of the table, a knife poised in one hand, ready to cut a big slice for somebody, when she stopped and stared.

Everybody followed her line of vision into the living room.

"I know what it is," she said, gawking at the bronze sculpture in the corner. "I swear to Betsy, I been lookin' at that darn thing all day and I finally figgered it out. I did."

They all waited, suspended, poised as if on the brink of some great scientific discovery. Matty Rae had figured it out. She was fixing to speak.

"Why, shoot," she said with a snort. "It's a tree! It's a Christmas tree!"

Leah looked over at the other tree, the real one beside it. The smell of cedar filled the house, and its colorful lights flickered at the end of each branch. Pop and Spencer had spent an entire evening stringing popcorn while she and Mark hung her handmade ornaments.

She reached for Mark's hand again and said for his ears only, "I love the tree."

He squeezed her hand tightly, smiled, and said, "Which one?" But he knew. He knew.

Have You Ever Wondered If You Could Write A Harlequin Novel?

Here's great news—Harlequin is offering a series of cassette tapes to help you do just that. Written by Harlequin editors, these tapes give practical advice on how to make your characters—and your story— come alive. There's a tape for each contemporary romance series Harlequin publishes.

Mail order only

All sales final
